PRAISE FOR FOR *YEA*

"This arousing novel celebrates feminine sexuality through one of the most original adventures of self-discovery written. The primary character – Dana – is surviving her first romantic breakup and the manner in which she not only survives but prospers and grows makes for one of the strongest Chick Lit novels to surface in quite a while."
    - Grady Harp, Top 100 Amazon Reviewer

"I think everyone will recognize a little of themselves in this book. It's laugh-out-loud funny, it's courageous, it's exhilarating. It's all the things you wished you'd done and some of the things you wish you hadn't. I can't wait to see what Lieberman follows this up with."
    - Award-Winning Author JP McLean

"A masterful, sensual, and humorously entertaining read, author Jennifer Lieberman's "Year of the What?", is a must-read novel of 2021! The character growth and humor really draw the reader in, and the overall theme of female sexuality and freedom really made this story feel both relevant and innovative in the face of a history of male sexual oppression. If you haven't yet, be sure to grab your copy today!"
    - Anthony Avina, Author, Blogger

"Because, if you are going to tell the truth, or something of value, you have to be willing to ruffle feathers, and rock boats, even if that means being misunderstood, and Jennifer Lieberman starts off her book with surfing waves…"
    - Scribble's Worth Book Reviews

"Don't read this in public…It will take you on a journey that will fuel your own sexual fantasies, experiences and future plans. Jennifer's writing presents a fully fleshed-out (!) exploration of female sexuality and pleasure, mixed with some painful and relatable misadventures too."
    -Barry Selby, #1 Best Selling Author of *50 Ways To Love Your Love*

"Year of the Slut leaves you wanting more - and in more ways than one!! I didn't want to put the book down and didn't want it to end..."
 - Ashley Gianni, Actress and Producer

"I look forward to the major motion picture as the writing screams BLOCKBUSTER HIT!!! Can't recommend this enjoyable read enough!"
 - Juan Carlos Miguel, Award-Winning Film and Theatre Director

"Even though it's not about science, there are no monsters, and nobody uses a lightsaber, I have really enjoyed this book! Just how much I've enjoyed it is quite a pleasant surprise! A girlie sex novel? I didn't think this book was even meant for blokes. Well, it's not. It's for everyone."
 - Jackson Baker, Actor

"...It's just plain fun! I loved following Dana from misadventure to misadventure and watching her change as a character. This is a funny, sexy page turner that I think you'll enjoy!"
 - Will Link, Author *Crazy About Kurt*

"Freedom is power. Women have always been told to be ashamed of their sexuality. This book must be read by all."
 - Bijou, Actress

"A feminine novel that every man should read, I liked it from the beginning to the end."
 - David V.

"It reminds me of a cross between 50 Shades of Grey and Sex in the City as far as the characters go but exhibits a quality of writing that provides amazing imagery bringing excitement to the reader and creates the need to read the next chapter. Well done!"
 - Betsy T.

Year of the What?

Year of the What?

A True Story…Kinda

Adapted from the Award-Winning
Solo Show *Year of the Slut*

Jennifer Lieberman

Maple Mermaid Publishing Corp.

DEDICATION

For everyone out there looking for love…
first you must find yourself.

TABLE OF CONTENTS

DEC|USED

"Who the fuck is Candice?"

It was 10:38 p.m. on a Tuesday night in early December.

Curled up, naked on the bed, soggy and drained. Alone in a cramped, dimly lit, boutique hotel room in Manhattan, I sobbed. My stomach tight in knots, throat closed and skin clammy. Mascara running down my face, staining the crumpled white linens as the painted tear drops fell. I was still covered with Russell and strangled by one thought, choking on it, nauseous and gasping…my insides at a crossroads between implosion and volcanic eruption. My body shook as my thoughts wailed…

"Who the fuck is Candice!"

I crawled over to the mini-bar and swallowed a mini-bottle of vodka. I relished the sting as it went down and quickly reached for another. As the mini-bottles of poison swam through my veins I pulled myself together and called Kelly. She would be over in twenty minutes. I took another bottle, I think it was rum that time, sucked it back slowly, desperate to put out the fire that was burning my insides. I stumbled into the shower to wash the past hour away. To wash Russell off of me.

Kelly arrived as I was getting out of the shower. I answered the door naked. She wrapped her arms around me, then rolled in the room with two large suitcases. I gazed at them as I collapsed onto the bed, whining, with another mini bottle in hand.

As always, Kelly didn't hold back, despite my fragile and naked state. "I'm actually happy this happened," she said with a smile as she opened one of the suitcases, which happened to be empty.

She filled it with items from the room: pillows, alarm clock, lamp, towels, toilet paper, basically anything that would fit in the suitcases. "Now you can finally move on from Russell. For good. You've wasted over four years on the guy, two too many in my opinion." Kelly continued around the room, searching for items to fill her bags.

"Are we stealing, is that what you brought the suitcases for?"

"It's not stealing, they have Russell's credit card number...they'll charge him for everything," she said casually, raising her eyebrows and flashing a devilish grin.

~ ~ ~ ~ ~ ~

Kelly was a tall, curvy redhead from Texas with small breasts, infectious laughter and a 'the party comes with me' attitude. At 5'9" she possessed a striking 'suicide girl' beauty. We met working at a café in Hell's Kitchen the summer I finished university. The summer I moved to New York City from a small town in Canada. Two months after I got to the Big Apple, I took the room that opened up in her apartment around the corner from the cafe. Kelly was the most outrageous person I'd ever met...and I loved it!

She wasn't refined, but she was, in fact, a genius, at least according to her IQ score. She dabbled in photography and bisexuality and recreationally experimented with drugs and Mary Jane. She had a full scholarship to NYU and remained at the top of her class no matter how much she partied. She also had a lot of sex and was really free about it; still a virgin when I moved in, I was both inwardly intrigued and outwardly judgmental about her promiscuity. She was grounded and confident in her behavior, and my reactions of shock and condemnation rarely fazed her.

"Dana, sex is no big deal!" she would say. "I lost my virginity when I was fifteen on a school trip to the Museum. The thing about the first time is it sucks. You just gotta get it over with so the pressure is off and you can really start enjoying sex. It's like anything, you're not gonna be good at it your first time! You need to practice and practice, and you *totally* need a vibrator if you ever expect to cum. A guy will never be able to get you there unless he's going down on you and usually that's not always a guarantee. I have three vibrators. You can try one."

"Ewwww, I don't think those are for sharing!" I squealed.

There was always at least one vibrator on Kelly's bed at any given time, sometimes up to three. She was a big fan of the vibrator. She had a large one that plugged into the wall, a portable one that could travel in her bag, and a waterproof one for the bath. I never met anyone so serious about masturbation or orgasms in general.

A few weeks into living together she confided in me that she wasn't going back to school after the summer break. She had started working as a dominatrix and didn't think wasting her time in school was worthwhile anymore.

"You're kidding me, right?" I mom-ed all over her. She was one of the smartest people I knew. "I get you being into that sort of thing, but why do you need to quit school?" I pressed hard.

"I'm bored with classes, and with the whole academic lifestyle. It's just not for me right now. I can't be trapped in a lecture hall. These are my vital creative and exploratory years. I need to be free from the system."

"What about your scholarship?"

"I don't care. What's the point of me finishing school? Even if I graduate and get my degree, even if I get a master's degree, I will not be making the kind of money I make in that dungeon in Chelsea. Honey, I make lawyer money—over $300 for an hour session, plus tips! If these guys are stupid enough to waste their money, I'm sure as hell smart enough to take it," she explained casually.

I was having trouble processing the news. This was not what I signed up for when I moved in with Kelly. I was not prepared to be rooming with a dominatrix! I froze.

"Relax girl, I don't fuck them; I whip, spank, trample, torture, but I am no prostitute."

~ ~ ~ ~ ~

I reached over to the hotel mini bar, still naked and shot Kelly a look. "You want a drink?"

"I want more than a drink. We are going to teach that dick a lesson," she said as she picked up the phone and ordered a few bottles of Veuve then pulled out a baggy of blow and started cutting lines on the nightstand.

I couldn't help but laugh. Kelly was the only person I knew who could turn this devastation into debauchery.

"You broke up six months ago, you moved out of his place back into mine—it's way past time to move on!" Kelly picked up the phone and ordered more towels and mini shampoo bottles.

She was right, and Candice was apparently what needed to happen for me to snap out of this delusion; that Russell would change and we would end up happily ever after.

How could I have been so naive? I was so sure Russell brought me to the hotel so we could get back together. I thought we were finally going to get married now that his band had broken up and he didn't have to be on the road all the time. We'd lived together for three years, and we were together for almost four, but the last time we spoke was in the spring when I ended it with him over the phone, while his van was broken down somewhere near Portland, and he hadn't been home in two months.

"How did this even happen?" Kelly demanded, confused by the whole thing.

It was the middle of December when my need to be swept off my feet was having a tug of war with my need to get laid. I was starting to realize I had needs, sexually…and finding the *right* person to sleep with was turning out to be more challenging than anticipated. It had been over eight months since I'd had sex. Before Russell this wouldn't have been an issue because I had never had sex, so I didn't know what I was missing, but now, I needed it, like, to be able to function. My body craved physical attention and it was getting hard to focus.

Earlier that day I'd been at a meeting with my boss, Henry, at a property on Museum Mile overlooking Central Park. It was selling for over $14 million, which wasn't even that much for the neighborhood. I had been Henry's assistant for two years and had grown accustomed to getting glimpses into his world. He was a real estate mogul with several side ventures, including investing in startups, apps, restaurants, nightclubs and whatever he found interesting at the time. Henry was a George Clooney type in his mid-fifties, in great shape, with salt-and-pepper hair and silver blue eyes, and he always wore a suit. There's something about a man in a suit. He always flashed his gleaming smile and he had a graceful power about him. I got a hostess job at one of his restaurants shortly after I started dating Russell, who was working there as a bartender at the time.

I quickly moved up to manager the first year at the restaurant and developed a connection with Henry, while helping him plan a few private events at the location. After the third event was a huge success, he offered me a job working with him directly, as Executive Assistant, but more like for his whole life rather than any one particular business, so I got to learn a lot about everything he did. My job entailed a mix of his personal and professional needs. Some days I was picking up dry cleaning and making dinner reservations and others looking at multi-million-dollar properties and going to red carpet events. It was a sweet gig and Henry was a lot of fun to work for, and was totally handsome.

After the meeting I wandered around the city on my way home. The holidays were a few weeks away, and Manhattan was buzzing with Christmas music and decorations. I kept my chin up and tried to enjoy the beauty of the city this time of year, despite my loneliness. I walked home along Central Park South and down Fifth Avenue. I watched the horses pull the carriages along the street. I've always fantasized about a carriage ride through the park. Yes, it's cheesy, but it also seems so old fashioned and romantic...I was longing for some old-fashioned romance, and let's be honest, some hot sex.

As I walked slowly, admiring the light dusting of snow and the Christmas displays in the shop windows, a smile washed over my face. I finally felt free, happy, and light hearted for the first time in months...since the breakup. I smiled and twirled around gleefully; I was finally ready to face the world of dating again. I reminded myself that Russell wasn't *the one*; as a struggling musician, he would never be able to give me the life I wanted or deserved. Not that I was look-ing for someone like Henry, but something between impoverished and impeccable would be a good start.

I walked down Fifth Avenue and stopped in some of the fancy couture shops, Gucci, Versace, Tiffany's...imagining what it would be like to be a wealthy Manhattan wife.

I made my way over to Ninth Avenue as the sprinkle of snow coated the city. I stopped off for an indulgence I could afford at my favorite vegan place tucked away on the corner of 47th Street and

Ninth Ave. I treated myself to a delish dinner of sizzling seitan and macro-greens, then ordered a slice of carrot cake to go.

It was after seven o'clock when I got to the apartment in Hell's Kitchen, and Kelly was rushing out to see her latest fling at a poetry slam on the Bowery.

Once Kelly left, I snuggled on the couch with the vegan carrot cake and scrolled my options to Netflix and chill with myself. I was happy to have a quiet night in.

My cell rang. I didn't recognize the number. I picked up anyway. "Hello."

"Hey there pretty baby."

My heart dropped to the floor and splattered. It was Russell. I should have hung up. But I didn't. I wanted to hear his voice. I wanted to know how he was. When I finally moved out of our basement in Queens six months ago, I never expected we would turn into complete strangers.

"Hi." I tried not to let him hear whatever feelings were flooding through my body.

"I miss you," he said.

My heart was beating so hard I was sure he could hear it on the other end of the phone. "I didn't recognize the number."

He laughed. "Yeah, I got a new phone. It's an LA number. I ended up staying there for a few months after the band broke up. I got a job at the record label that signed Louis." I was trying to listen, but my heart kept missing beats and I was feeling light-headed. "Can you believe I have a grown-up job now? And a place in SoHo?"

SoHo? Wow, he must be doing really well. I started having visions of our future together. Despite everything my mother said about him being some bum in a band, I always believed in him. "I'm sorry about the way things ended. So much shit was going down with the band

7

falling apart, I felt like…a loser…watching seven years of hard work go down the drain," he confessed.

He never shared any of that with me when we were together. I wished he had been able to talk to me about it. I also understood that when you feel like your life is falling apart it's pretty impossible to keep it together for anyone else. Maybe he needed me to walk away so he could find his new path. I needed to walk away to find mine. And here we were months later on the phone. Maybe we found our way back to each other?

~ ~ ~ ~ ~

One night that first summer with Kelly she dragged me out to the Lower East Side to The Bowery Ballroom, where her friend's band was playing. A few drinks in I couldn't help noticing the music from this other band; well, my ass couldn't help it. When it comes to good music, my ass has a mind of its own. I got close to the stage and felt flush, as the musical vibrations filled my chest cavity and resonated throughout my body. Each note, each key, each strum of his guitar tickled me from the inside. My body whipped back and forth, humping the air as if there were bodies rubbing against me. I don't know if it was the song or the way he licked the sweat from the top of his lip as he strummed his guitar, but suddenly it all clicked. He had brown hair and big brown eyes and I wanted to vomit when he came over to talk to me after his set.

"I loved watching you dance," he said.

I nearly fell over. Kelly caught me.

"I'm Russell." He grinned at me with his big puppy eyes and his crooked smile and he swept his sweaty brown hair back with his left hand.

I was frozen. Kelly swooped in and invited him to a party we were all of the sudden having at our place the next night.

We didn't say much before our lips found each other. Before I knew it Russell and I were making out in the alley as his band loaded their van. We kissed viciously behind the club; he tore my shirt and I couldn't get enough. He was a sexy guitar player. My heart flooded; blood rushed through my veins. Russell sucked on my earlobe and grazed his fingertips over my nipples as my legs trembled. I peeled myself off of him and caught my breath for a few moments as I watched their van pull away.

Shit! I'd never had a party before, like one that my mom didn't plan for me, and only had a few hours to pull it off. Kelly and I baked, blended, chopped and mixed like culinary queens, then took it all up to the roof, which was the only place with enough space for everyone. Since we lived on the top floor of the building, we considered the roof an extension of our apartment.

Two hours in, Kelly had changed her outfit at least three times, and by this point declared it a lingerie party; she convinced everyone to strip down to their undies. The ninety-degree heat was unrelenting. You could see steam rising up from the city, bodies were moist and feverish, so we kept the Jell-O shots and slushy margaritas flowing at a constant pace. It was almost ten o'clock and Russell still hadn't shown. I didn't know what was making me more nauseous, the idea of him coming or the idea of him not coming. I went downstairs to my room to see if there were any messages on my cell. None. Just then I heard the sweetest sound in the entire world.

"Hey pretty baby! I've been looking for you," he said in his deep voice.

I blushed. "Hi."

"Cool place," he said as he looked around the room.

I jumped up anxiously. "Wait until you see the roof."

Russell leaned in to kiss me. He wrapped his arms around me, holding ever so tightly; my body relaxed into his chest and we kissed

9

for a few minutes before I took him up. It didn't take long before he found himself a guitar and began playing while leaning along the edge of the brick wall with the Manhattan skyline lit up behind him. The rest of the party pretty much fell away once Russell arrived. I was lost in his eyes, his music, and the sweet sound in his voice when he called me *pretty baby*. Kelly and I danced the night away as the lights of the city glowed in the background.

By 3:00 a.m. mostly everyone had cleared out. Russell and I headed down to the apartment. I was nervous to have a strange boy in my room and was heading into unchartered territory. I wasn't sure how old Russell was, but it was apparent he had close to a decade on me. We both sat awkwardly on the edge of my bed.

"Thanks for inviting me, it was a fun party," he said.

The tension between us was electrifying. Russell leaned in and stole a quick kiss. I closed my eyes and could taste the beer on his lips.

"This was my first party," I whispered.

Russell tenderly stroked my cheek and kissed me again, much deeper, much harder. I fell back on the bed and he fell with me. We rolled around on my single mattress, making out hard, hands wandering over chests, arms, and thighs.

"Wait." I abruptly blocked his hand as it was making its way up my skirt. "It's pretty late, Russell. Don't you think you should be heading home?"

"I don't have a curfew," he joked. "Do you need to be up for work or something?"

"No," I hesitated.

"So, what's the problem? Don't you want me to stay?" He looked into my eyes.

I went into a full-on emotional panic. I'd never spent the night with a guy before, except for Sean, my best friend from back home. I was terrified. Obviously, sex would be expected, and I still wasn't ready for that, and if Russell knew the truth, that I was saving myself for *the one*, would he even want to stick around? I was overwhelmed. Tears streamed down my cheeks.

I felt like such a loser. I was almost twenty-one, a grown adult with a BA, living on my own in the coolest city in the world, and I couldn't handle spending the night alone with a guy? The reality of being alone in my room with a guy I just met, who obviously wanted to have sex, was frightening.

Russell was staring at me so intently that I was afraid he'd look too closely and see my acne scars, that my eyes are too close together, and my nose…I was afraid that he would see all the things I didn't like about myself. No one had ever reassured me that my flaws were what made me beautiful. I wouldn't realize this until years later, when Russell's crooked tooth would be what I loved most about his looks.

"Uhh, you don't need to cry." Russell stood up and started fixing his hair nervously. "I'll get out of here …" He crossed to the door.

Suddenly, Kelly pounded on the door, completely wasted. "Are you finally losing your virginity in there? I really hope so, Dana!" she cackled in drunken laughter.

Humiliated, I crumbled and buried my face in my pillow, completely paralyzed. Russell sat down next to me, now understanding my teary outburst. "Baby, hey, look at me."

It took me several minutes before I could look up at him with my soggy, red face. He sat there waiting, caressing my head until I did.

"Hey, I'm just getting to know you. I'm not expecting anything tonight. I just thought it would be nice to hold you in my arms until the sun came up, then take you to brunch."

I looked into his big puppy eyes and crooked smile that coaxed his dimples.

"I would really like that," I said, blushing.

11

Russell and I curled up on my bed together fully clothed and I melted into the warmth of his body, inhaled his clean laundry scent, and slept in his arms all night. I had never felt more special.

~ ~ ~ ~ ~

That evening, after hearing what he went through on the road with his band falling apart, I was almost able to forgive him for being such an asshole. I felt bad I wasn't more sympathetic to how hard he had it. I thought he was pulling away because he lost interest in me. Plus I had suspicions of him cheating. I let my insecurities get the best of me, when he was going through his own drama.

"Have dinner with me," he said.

"Okay," I whispered.

After I hung up the phone, I felt like he was still the guy I fell in love with four years ago. I wanted to see him. I also really needed to have sex, and Russell was still the only guy I had ever slept with. I decided Russell was safe, not for my mental health, but for my stats; sleeping with him my number wouldn't increase, so it would be as if it didn't count. And who knew, now that he was working at a record label managing artists, living in a loft in SoHo, maybe he finally was ready to give me everything he couldn't before...in the basement in Queens.

We were supposed to meet at 6:00 p.m. and go to dinner somewhere overlooking Central Park. At 5:30 p.m. he cancelled on dinner because he ran late at a meeting. He updated me with texts every so often and was finally ready to see me close to nine o'clock.

We met in the lobby of a boutique hotel on Central Park at 9:15. He was holding a greasy brown paper bag with Chinese takeout. "I got us a room," he grinned.

We were silent in the elevator, keeping our distance, staring each other up and down. He was wearing a suit. I had never seen him in a suit. I didn't even know he owned one. He looked beautiful. He had chopped off his long brown hair and shaved off his scruff. His big brown puppy eyes were smiling at me. He looked the cleanest I had ever seen him. He probably smelled the best, too, like expensive cologne. I was wearing a short red dress and black boots. He pulled my hat off in the elevator with his free hand. My long wavy chestnut locks stood up from static. I had dark eyeliner around my hazel eyes and gobs of lip gloss on.

"You're wearing a lot of makeup," he said as he reached out his hand and lifted up my chin, studying me.

He was right. I was wearing more makeup than he'd probably ever seen on me. I wanted to look hot. I wanted to look sexy. I wanted him to want me. I wanted him to see me as new and exciting.

When we got into the room the bag of Chinese food barely hit the floor and his pants were already at his ankles. Before I knew what was going on he had me flat on my back on the bed. He collapsed onto me, deeply inhaling the scent of my hair, then kissing up my neck. I missed his smell, his taste, his touch, his breath sending chills through me. Emotions flooded through my insides. His touch was familiar and comforting. He gently grabbed a fistful of my hair, and I let out a tiny gasp. He knew how to drive me wild, how to make me moan *please,* quietly begging for him.

"Wait a second…" I gasped. Things were moving much faster than I anticipated.

"Can we slow down and just talk for a bit? I haven't seen you in a really long time…"

"Um, sure, what did you want to talk about?" he muttered as he pulled off my boots one at a time.

I held my ground. "I'm serious. I'm happy you brought me here, but this is moving too fast." I didn't just want to get laid because it had been eight months since I'd felt a man's touch; I wanted Russell.

I wanted to feel the way only he knew how to make me feel...safe and protected and loved.

Russell played confused, unzipped my jacket, and grabbed a handful of my left breast. "Fast? Babe, we've already done this like hundreds of times…"

"Slow down! I'm serious. You're trying to get my clothes off and you haven't even kissed me."

Russell slowly pulled his hands away from me and we sat up on the bed. He avoided looking at me. "I'm sorry," he whispered.

I gently took his face in my hands, looked him deep in the eyes and kissed him softly. He kissed me back but that spark I remembered was missing. Something had changed.

He pulled my dress off and climbed on top of me, pinning my wrists above my head with one hand and removing my black lace panties with the other. He guided himself into me and I was so overwhelmed I wasn't even thinking about a condom. I gasped as he pushed his way deeper than I was expecting.

"Ouch!" I pushed him back slightly.

"Are you okay?" He paused, looking down at me.

"I haven't…it's been a while." I stared into his eyes, telling him what I meant without saying it. That he was still the only one. He smiled, kissed me, and continued. He lowered his body onto mine and he arrived almost instantly, pouring himself over my chest before I even had a chance to feel anything other than a sharp pain, and then he collapsed next to me. I kissed his shoulder while stroking his head, confused and even more sexually frustrated than when I got there.

As I lay on the white hotel sheets, contemplating what just happened, Russell came out of the bathroom toweling himself off. He kissed my forehead. My body longed in anticipation, waiting for him to lie next to me and wrap me in his arms as we slept intertwined.

"That was just as good as I remember," he said grinning.

"Yeah?" I questioned—he was kidding, right?

He turned away, put on his pants and searched for his shirt.

"What about dinner?" I asked.

"I've gotta run, babe, you enjoy it."

"What do you mean? You can't stay?"

"The room is yours until morning…watch a movie, have fun!"

"By myself?"

He didn't respond.

"I don't understand."

His eyes darted away from me.

"When do I get to see you again?"

He dashed around the small room, slipped on his watch, shirt, jacket, tie. He slid his feet into his shoes one at a time and backed up towards the door. "Babe, you know I love you, just the timing isn't right yet. I've got some really great momentum with work now. I can't slow down. I'm too crazy about you; if we were together, I wouldn't get anything done. Shit, you know what you do to me…I can't keep my pants on when I'm near you…I'm with Candice now because she doesn't get in my way."

He swaggered out the door with his shirt unbuttoned, tie opened and one sock missing.

"Candice! Who the fuck is Candice? And don't you just love how he slipped that in just as he was creeping out the door … we didn't even use a condom. I'm such an idiot."

Kelly sympathized with me while stuffing the extra towels she had called for and the last of the snacks from the mini bar in the second suitcase.

"Dana, did you really think you could just come here and have sex with Russell and poof, you'd all of a sudden be back together?" Kelly scolded me.

"Well, kinda." I looked down, realizing how silly it sounded out loud.

"Really?" she stared me down. "It didn't have anything to do with the fact that you're a virgin once removed, you haven't fucked in forever, and you're afraid to have sex with anyone new, so you needed to take care of business with your ex, the only guy who's ever been inside you?"

"Maybe a little bit…" I hated that Kelly was always right.

"I'm not saying he isn't a total dick for the way he treated you and cheated on his new thing or whatever, but you are over Russell. He's not *the one*."

I was lounging across the bed, slightly drunk, wrapped in a hotel robe as the room service cart pushed through the door. Kelly was done packing up the contents of the room and quickly rolled the cart next to the bed and shut the door. She popped open a bottle of bubbly as I grabbed a jumbo shrimp and dipped it in cocktail sauce. Kelly sprayed champagne all over us on the bed. I giggled as I licked the liquid off my hands. Kelly poured herself a glass as she sat down to enjoy a selection of the most expensive menu items. I grabbed the bottle of bubbles off the cart and started swigging large gulps while splashes trickled down my neck, chest, and torso.

After enjoying the food and polishing off the first bottle of champagne, Kelly got some music going and we had a pillow fight/dance party jumping on the bed, tearing up the room. During the celebration to conclude the Russell Saga that was my life, the hotel room declined into disaster. Curtains were pulled off the windows, the legs of the bed collapsed, food and empty bottles covered the floor, tables were overturned. I don't remember how it all happened, but I will never forget what the room looked like when we left.

"Russell will never talk to me again after this," I slurred to Kelly as she dragged me out of the room at 5:00 a.m.

"Good! That was the plan," she snapped.

My eyes swelled with tears, accepting the finality of it all. Kelly squeezed me hard.

"You did him a favor…he's gotta leave a few trashed hotel rooms in his path if he ever expects to earn a Grammy…" she winked.

We laughed and headed home along Ninth Avenue rolling two gigantic suitcases with us. Sure, I was pissed at Russell, but ugly truths began surfacing that night, ones I was reluctant to face. After all the work and time I put in to *us*, where was *I?* Left dwelling on the past and the pain, still asking myself, *will anyone ever love me again?* I had only myself to blame.

"Don't worry Dana. I have a feeling twenty-five is gonna be your *Year of the Slut.*"

I looked at her, puzzled. "Year of the WHAT?" I questioned.

"The year you realize you're spending your hottest years being a prude, and start making up for lost time before it's too late and you're settled in a white-picket prison in suburbia with two-point-five snot monsters controlling your life. If you don't start having sex for yourself now, when will you ever do it?"

As much as I didn't want to hear it, my brilliant and crazy friend did have a point.

JAN | THE MOVIE STAR

"You're in love with Beth?"

My face scrunched up as I tried not to show my disappointment. Beth was the lead actress in the movie I was working on. All the guys were drooling over her. She was blonde, blue-eyed, 5'7" and skinny, but curvy in the right places. Fine, she was hot, but I didn't see what the big deal was because she was kind of a bitch…And after two hours of professional hair styling and makeup applications anyone could look like a supermodel, or pretty close to it.

"She's beautiful," I told Rey, because I knew that's what he wanted to hear.

"She's my mission for the remainder of the shoot," he stated, staring out into the night.

It was the middle of January and it had been a month since the Russell disaster. I started the New Year determined to get back on track with my own life and stop worrying about a relationship or lack thereof. I landed a small role working on an independent horror film that started shooting the second week of January. On my last day, well, my only day of work, I overheard the producer say they were shorthanded in the art department. I saw my opportunity and offered to work behind the scenes. The producer agreed and I was hired to stay on for the remainder of the shoot. My job consisted of dressing the set, gathering props, making fake blood, and basically doing whatever they needed.

My real boss, Henry the mogul, loved me, so he let me take the three weeks off from my assistant job to work on the movie. He knew acting was my dream and being a dreamer himself he was never one to stand in the way of dreams. He also happened to be in St. Barts for an impromptu getaway with his latest model/girlfriend, so it was a good time to ask for a favor.

The movie was a low budget horror film shooting on a farm upstate. There was a main house, a large barn, and a few cabins and sheds scattered around the four acres. The property was lovely covered in snow, but, once the sun went down, the place felt really creepy, with dilapidated barns and rotted trees leaning lopsided, casting weird shadows. It was the perfect setting for a horror flick.

I reported to Asher, the production designer; he had dirty blond hair, brown eyes, and was cute in a scruffy puppy kind of way. He made it clear he was into me, but I had my eye on Rey, the production manager. Rey was a tall, dark, Puerto Rican hottie, more built and muscular than Asher and, in general, just seemed to bathe more frequently. He was also an actor and did theater in the city, so he and I had something in common.

The days were long and grueling for everyone. Asher was constantly giving me hugs and encouragement. Rey became a shoulder to lean on as we both commiserated over our recent breakups and move-outs while we smoked weed in his car after we wrapped each night. He drove me home a few times when we stayed late cleaning up, assuring me driving through Hell's Kitchen was on his way home to New Jersey.

One night on the drive home I confided in Rey, "I wrote a play and was thinking of submitting it for a reading at the theater company I'm part of," I said, half proud and half embarrassed.

"Oh, yeah," he perked up.

"It's a short one-act with two characters, male and female. Would you, maybe, want to read it with me sometime? It's never been read aloud before." I thought Rey would be great to play opposite me. I also hoped my play could be a way to spend time with him. I was starting to really like him.

"I want to read it," he said, leaning across me to open my door. "Bring it down. I'll wait in the car."

"Now?" I was surprised at his interest.

He nodded. I darted up the six flights of stairs, printed a copy, and ran it down to his parked, black Eclipse.

A few days went by and he never mentioned my play. I knew he had a lot on his plate with the film, so I didn't bug him. He was the only person I'd given it to, other than Kelly, and I was nervous about what he might think. Maybe he thought it sucked, because he never mentioned it again, and neither did I. I felt stupid for sharing it with him.

Beth's smoking-hot body and pouty lips weren't the only things causing a stir on set. It turned out she didn't have the best attitude. She was continuously late, never knew her lines, and never wore a bra. No one on the overwhelmingly male crew seemed to have issues with any of that. If they did, they never said anything. Even Rey was completely hypnotized—he didn't even get mad when her cell phone rang while the cameras were rolling, which is one of the biggest taboos on a film shoot.

I couldn't understand how she could get such a big part and I got killed off in the first scene? Okay, fine, once you get over the whole blonde Kardashian thing, what was there? Why would they put up with someone so unprofessional when I was sitting right here and willing to work really hard? Then it occurred to me…her role was topless. I didn't want to be considered for any of the topless roles.

The fact that I had more self-respect than Beth (or more insecurity about being nude) did not make me feel better; I was jealous of her, plain and simple. I've never been one of those girls who just walks into a room and everyone notices. At 5'4", with an athletic build, hazel eyes, and wavy chestnut-brown hair, I was super active, but not obsessive. Beth had perfect skin and her hair was never out of place, not even when she was covered in fake blood. Her voice was deep and raspy and the way she swung her ass when she walked made the entire crew weak at the knees.

"She smells like peaches," Rey would whisper every time her scent wafted by him.

This girl oozed sex appeal. I wished I could be *that*. Sure, I had more confidence and style than when I was in high school, but I didn't have that wow factor, no matter how badly I wanted it. And I had no idea how to get it.

The movie only had one real star, well, he was an up and coming, Trevor Stone. His work had gotten a lot of press at Sundance and Tribeca last year. He went to film school with the director, so they were able to get him without paying him his usual rate. They flew him in from LA so the entire shoot was scheduled around his availability. The day Trevor arrived everyone was buzzing with energy. For most of us it was our first film so we could barely contain ourselves in the presence of a real celebrity—even the guys were excited. His looks didn't hurt either. He was a quiet, African American guy with a calm but powerful presence.

I couldn't believe I was working on a film with an actual Hollywood star! I grew up in a small town in Ontario, Canada, and my best friend, Sean, and I had dreamed of making movies and moving to Hollywood together ever since I could remember … so he could make the movies and I could star in them. He said I inspired his vision. We had been writing and performing skits in my backyard since we were kids, and by high school we were shooting shorts on his dad's camera. He went to film school at the University of Toronto and I studied marketing at York University, because my parents didn't consider a degree in Theater useful (they were in total denial). We became serious collaborators on his film projects through university; I continued to be his inspiration, and one of our films even got into a few film festivals, giving us a glimpse of what our future would be like. It was pretty exciting. Now I was on an actual movie set in New York City with an actual star. I had to pinch myself.

Trevor had a strong "CrossFit" body and light brown eyes. He was 5"9 and had perfect teeth and a shy, sexy smile. From his looks, you would think he was a total asshole, but, as it turned out, he was one of the nicest guys there, friendly and polite to everyone. He had zero attitude and a quiet confidence I admired.

Beth declared Trevor was hers early on in the shoot, before she had ever met him, and now that he had arrived she wasn't going to let anyone get in her way. She was half interested in him, but mostly interested in the press she could get being on his arm. He wasn't a major movie star yet, but he was famous enough to get his picture snapped at the grocery store from time to time.

Trevor had a trailer in his contract, so the production rented one only for the time he was in town. Beth was somehow under the impression that it was also her trailer and was constantly in Trevor's face. The poor guy couldn't go anywhere without her on his trail.

The movie star requested assistance going over his lines so Rey volunteered me for the position. I was thrilled to have the chance to spend time with him. I knew Rey wasn't being nice; he was being strategic, trying to keep Beth away from Trevor to protect his own interests. I didn't care; it worked out great for me.

There I was at Trevor's trailer. It was just an RV, not a fancy one like on the big studio movies. There was a kitchen with a table, a bathroom with a shower, and a bed at the back with a curtain you could pull across for privacy.

"Hi, I'm Dana. I'm here to run lines," I said quietly when he opened the door.

"Hey. Great. Come on in." Trevor cleared his bag and his jacket to make room for me to sit in the banquet in the kitchen.

"So, where do you want to go from?" I asked nervously, flipping through my script.

"We can take a minute before we dive in." He smiled.

Trevor was genuine and easy to talk to. We talked about our respective hometowns. He told me about living in LA. I told him about New York life. We compared the bands we liked. I soon realized he didn't want to go over lines at all; he just wanted someone to talk to. I wasn't blind to the fact that he was gorgeous, but after working for Henry, I was in contact with so many celebrities, from millionaires to moguls, that I could see them all as people.

"Hello there, anybody home?" Beth burst in with her smoky voice.

Trevor stood up and went to the door to block her from coming in.

"Hey Beth." He greeted her in an annoyed tone.

"What-cha doin' in here? Taking a nap? Do you want me to come snuggle with you?" she asked and put her arms around him, leaning over his shoulder. She peered inside and noticed me at the table then pulled off of him quickly.

"What's she doing here?" she snapped in a catty tone.

"She's helping me run lines. Mind coming back later?" Trevor replied.

"I can do that with you!" She slithered up to him seductively.

He took both of her hands in his and said, "Sweetheart, you're talent. You shouldn't bother yourself with that stuff."

Beth was both flattered and disappointed. She tossed her hair seductively and pranced away without a fuss.

Trevor and I went back to chatting.

"How did you get involved in the production? Did you go to film school?" he asked.

"No, I'm an actress. I had a small role and got killed off the first week," I explained. "I want to learn what happens on a movie set, so here I am…"

His gaze pierced through me. "Smart."

"I wrote a play," I said. "I want to be more than an actor."

"Can I read it? Will you bring me a copy?" he asked curiously.

"Sure," I lied. If Rey couldn't be bothered to read my stuff, there was no way this guy would, so I spared myself the humiliation.

Dodging Beth became a full-time job for Trevor, which was pretty funny to watch, considering she had every guy eating out of the palm of her hand, except the one she wanted. It seems that cruel humor of life strikes against all women, no matter where we stand on the hotness scale.

I became Trevor's go-to person for running lines each day, even though we rarely looked at the script. On Trevor's fifth day shooting, I brought breakfast and coffee to his trailer. My greasy, unwashed hair was hidden under a wool hat; I was on my fifth day without a shower. I unzipped my fleece hoodie and rested it over the bench; my gray thermal hugging my body.

"Morning superstar," I whispered, peeking in at him lying on the bed in the back through the crack in the curtain. "I brought coffee and a breakfast sandwich."

"Thanks, darlin'. Just put it down, I need to lie here for a few," he mumbled between the pillows.

"Sure thing. I'll come back in twenty."

"Stay. Chill. I like having you around. Just make sure no one bugs me."

Ten minutes later Trevor emerged and sat next to me, picked up his cup of coffee, took a sip, and let out a sigh. He looked at me long and hard for a moment, the morning sun streamed in through the fogged-up windows. It was freezing outside.

"You're really beautiful, you know," he stated, simply.

I was caught by surprise, un-slept and unwashed. It had been a long time since I'd received a compliment from a sexy guy.

"You walk around here with no makeup, a fuzzy hat and baggy clothes, but I can still see it," he said almost critically, like it irritated him that I didn't try harder.

"You know what these days are like; I haven't showered since my last day off, before you even started," I said a little defensively.

"I wasn't criticizing you, I was just saying, no matter how much you're trying to cover it up, I can see you. Plus, you have a good heart. I can tell," he said sweetly.

"Thanks," I smiled, a bit confused.

"No boyfriend?"

I shook my head, no. He leaned in and kissed me softly on the lips.

I abruptly stood up.

"I, ah, totally forgot, I need to fill a bunch of prosthetics with blood bags for the massacre this afternoon. I've, ah, gotta go." I darted out of there.

That was my first kiss since Russell. I avoided Trevor for the rest of the day.

That night, Trevor somehow ended up in Rey's car for our drive back to the city. Trevor was staying at a hotel in Times Square a few blocks from my apartment. The three of us went for drinks in Trevor's hotel bar. We all had too much. Trevor asked me up to his room to take care of some bloody shirts for him; I nodded and followed. It was part of my job. Rey plopped himself on a couch in the lobby as we headed to the room.

Trevor held the door open and entered the hotel room behind me.

"You're adorable. I just wanted to get you alone." He laughed, slurring his words. He kissed his way from my shoulder up my neck, and then nibbled on my ear as his hands wandered up my shirt.

"I can't, I'm sorry." I pulled away from him. "Trevor, I am really flattered and definitely attracted to you…"

"Good," he cut me off.

"But…"

"There is always a *but* with you good girls…" he teased.

"I've only been with one guy, and I'm still getting over it," I confessed. "I'm not ready to be with anyone else yet. And if I were it wouldn't be for a casual fuck. I don't even know you that well."

Trevor took my hand and sat down on the bed, pulling me towards him. "You know me better than the last few girls I've slept with."

"Then they weren't sleeping with you, they were banging your looks or your celebrity." I immediately felt bad for saying it.

Trevor looked down.

"You're right. You can see beyond that. I like you. You're smart. And I knew you wouldn't stay, but I had to ask." Looking into my eyes, he ran the back of his hand along my face and kissed me tenderly. For a few moments, I was lost in his kiss, his hands wandering over my belly, feeling over my breasts and lightly teasing my nipples. I hadn't been this aroused in months. I could feel a puddle collecting in my panties as pleasure washed over my body. I forced myself away from him.

"I have to get back, Rey is waiting."

"Let him wait," Trevor whispered as he licked my neck.

"See you tomorrow," I said quietly.

"Before you go, take a look at what you did to me." He took my hand and slid it over the bulge in his pants. Looking me in the eye, he said, "You did this," as he grinned and kissed me goodnight.

"So, you don't have any bloody shirts?"

We both smiled.

Rey was passed out on the couch when I got back to the hotel lobby and it took me a few minutes to get him up. We stumbled back to my apartment and I insisted he crash at my place. He was wasted. We stopped for a slice of pizza on the way and were almost sober by the time we settled into my room.

I changed into flannel pajama pants and a T-shirt in the bathroom. When I got back from washing up, Rey had stripped down to his boxers. His clothes were dirty from working and I didn't have anything that would fit him. I let him sleep in my bed with me. We were friends. We had spent weeks together talking every day. I trusted him … I also knew he wasn't remotely interested in me; his heart was set on Beth.

Lying there in the dark, I was far over on one side of the bed, my body running along the edge of the single mattress, giving Rey lots of room. After a few minutes, he rolled closer to me and asked, "Why are you so far away? Don't you wanna cuddle?"

Cuddle? Rey had a strong, muscular body. He also smelled really good all the time. Even after a long day. I figured he was probably as lonely as I was, still getting over his own recent breakup.

"Okay," I said softly.

He slid closer and pulled me in tight. I took a deep breath and let out a sigh. He felt good. After a couple of minutes intertwined, he began running his foot along the top of mine, then along my calf. I could feel his warm breath blowing past my ear as he exhaled. Then I could feel his lips running along my ear, and then turning into tiny kisses.

"Rey…" I whispered.

"Yeah," he replied.

"What are you doing?" I asked, almost moaning.

"Kissing your ear."

"Why?" I pressed.

"I know you like me. Isn't this what you wanted? This is why you insisted I stay."

His hands wandered down to my stomach and started making their way up my shirt. I sat up quickly.

"No. That is not why I suggested you stay! You're too drunk to drive, I couldn't let you get behind the wheel. And maybe I do have a crush on you, but you're clearly not into me," I snapped.

"Says who?" he questioned.

"Says you in the ten million conversations we've had about how much you want Beth."

"Oh, right." He took a minute to think of something to say. "We can still make each other feel good…"

Really? This is the guy I'd been crushing on? I didn't want to be some drunken consolation because Beth wasn't interested. The next person I slept with was going to be someone who saw me as the prize.

"I'll see you in the morning."

I got up and crept into Kelly's room. She was still awake reading in bed.

"Can I sleep with you tonight?" I whispered sadly.

"Sure thing." She scooched over and pulled the covers back to let me in.

My friendship with Rey was all fucked up. We barely said two words to each other the rest of the shoot and the entire crew could tell something was up since we were no longer buddy-buddy. They all assumed we finally slept together. It turns out sleeping with someone isn't the only #1 fastest way to ruin a friendship; apparently rejection is tied in that #1 spot.

Trevor finished up his last scenes on a Monday. We had a few more stolen moments and sultry kisses over his last week but I never let it go beyond that. Of course, I wanted to. He was sweet and sexy, but I knew once he left I would have felt lonelier. He gave me his number and e-mail and told me to give him a call when I got out to LA.

Just before he left his trailer for the last time, he handed me a gift bag filled with tissue paper. A beautiful blue leather notebook and a package of colored gel pens were inside, as well as a postcard of the sun setting over the Statue of Liberty. On the back the card read:

"Keep dreaming and keep writing...
xo Trevor
P.S. Love your play!"

It turned out his first day on set Trevor found the copy of the play I gave to Rey on a table; he picked it up, glanced at the cover page and decided to keep it for himself because the title intrigued him: *Stained: A Love Story*. He read it that day. Maybe his interest in me wasn't so random after all.

Trevor's encouragement gave me the confidence to forge ahead to *my* future ... I submitted *Stained* to the summer one-act festival at the Cherry Lane Theater. It was accepted.

FEB | KISSING KIMS

"Me? Reckless?!" I slurred, astonished as the ecstasy started to wear off.

I don't know exactly what happened, what was said, or what mode of transportation was used, but somehow, I showed up at Asher's loft party in Bushwick making out with Kym #2.

Something was off. Every time I tried to hook up with Asher I kept ending up severely intoxicated with my tongue in some Kim's mouth.

The girls I grew up with in a small-town Canadian suburb enjoyed listening to my escapades in the big city. Although mine were tame compared to Kelly's, I was the outrageous one to them. For me, their lives were so different from mine that it was refreshing hearing about who got into which law firm, who was getting hitched, preggers, and what people chose to put on the bridal/shower registry. Most of my friends from home were on their way down a solid career path. They were finishing up master's degrees in business and finance, graduating law school and beginning to break off into serious nesting couples on their way down the aisle and back to suburbia. Let's face it, although most of my girlfriends were bright and earned fancy degrees, all they truly wanted was to find *the one*, settle down, start families and never work the corporate grind.

When things fell apart with Russell, I had some serious anxiety about being way behind so many of my friends from home who were getting engaged. A couple of girls even had kids already. A few friends were getting on my case about moving home and finding someone legitimate to settle down with before it was *too late*. They questioned how much more time I'd *waste* with the silly theater thing anyway—until they heard the gossip about Trevor Stone, then all they wanted to talk about was how my life was such a cool adventure. The truth is I was only just starting to figure out who I was. I didn't have enough experience to make any real-life decisions yet, or even think of marriage.

The bar was loud and crowded for a Sunday night. There was a group around the pool table and both pinball machines were in use. The place had a retro feel and the DJ was spinning 90s alt rock. We had wrapped shooting the horror film earlier that night and, after I helped Asher load the props and equipment into the production van, he gave me a lift home. As we approached the bridge into the city, Asher suggested we grab a drink to celebrate our awesome work and my first job on a film, so we headed to Williamsburg.

I found a table while Asher got us a couple of drinks. He returned with two beers and two shots of tequila. We raised our tequila shots, clinked our glasses, and threw them back. I cringed at the taste. While we swigged our beer, chatting, I searched his face, his eyes, for some spark of attraction. Asher was interested in me, and I liked the attention, but I didn't really have any feelings for him in return...*Perfect!* I thought, *he's a nice enough guy, I find him attractive...Could he be someone to just fuck around with? No strings, no pain, no attachment?*

Two shots and two beers later I was past my limit, and felt something tickling along my neck. It took me a minute to notice someone was touching me. As I cocked my head to the right to see who it was, this girl's face dove right into mine, planting a sloppy wet kiss right on my lips. I couldn't see anything, I was buried in her auburn curly hair, but I knew that smell anywhere—Maker's Mark and Chanel No. 5. Kimberly!

Kimberly used to date Louis, the lead singer from Russell's band. She was an advertising executive and totally loaded, both rich and a lush. She gave the band money to pay for their first recordings before I ever met Russell. She was a high-powered suit during the day and a borderline alcoholic by night. I had to hand it to her, though; she never had a sip of the stuff during office hours.

We used to party together at her loft in Tribeca when I started dating Russell. She would get us all drunk, strip down to her naughty lingerie and then flirt with the other guys to make Louis jealous. I was convinced her favorite pastime was making men fight over her, so Russell and I stopped going over. It was too much drama and secretly we couldn't stand her. She was obnoxious and totally selfish. I hadn't seen her in at least two years.

I pulled my lips away from hers and wiped off her drool. "Kimberly? Shit, it's been a lifetime!"

"Yeah, I know. You still with Russell?"

I shook my head.

"Good, now we can hang out!"

She sauntered off to the bar and I had a chance to fill Asher in on who she was. She returned to the table with three shots of Maker's. I couldn't handle any more alcohol, but I was afraid of Kimberly so I did what she said. We all threw back a shot.

The rest of the night got off track from there. I remember Kimberly's smell in my nose and her taste in my mouth. We made out for a considerable amount of time while dancing and grinding to No Doubt before Asher was able to pry us apart. I had her number written on my arm in pen the next morning, yet no intention of ever calling her.

I don't know how I ended up making out with her that night. I didn't even like her; why did I kiss her? I'm sure Asher wasn't upset with the show, but it was so out of character for me. The first time Asher and I got to hang out away from work and all of the sudden I was into girls? When did I become a lesbian?

Asher helped me stumble back to the van parked in an alley a few blocks away. The crisp, February air was refreshing; drunk at two in the morning, I was flushed and dizzy as the world spun and the traffic lights glowed. Asher helped me into the front row of the van so I could lie down; as he leaned over, I pulled him on top of me and started kissing him. I was drunk and horny and didn't care about meaning or consequence. I wanted to get fucked hard and dirty in the van. I wasn't thinking about intimacy as I felt his throbbing erection against my pelvic bone. What I was experiencing was pure and primal.

Asher pulled himself off of me, turned around, shut the door and returned to my lips. His body pressed against mine as we lay across the row of seats. He traced the outline of my face with his lips, kissing my cheek ever so lightly. I wrapped my legs around his waist and grinded my body against his aggressively. The alcohol had taken me over; I was out of control, and all my suppressed sexual cravings were surfacing, with a guy I wasn't even sure I liked. My body was overtaken by sensations and I surrendered to them. For the first time, I let go.

The windows fogged up and the van was steamy. We were layered for the season and struggled to get our jackets and sweaters off. The heat of our bodies met with the chill in the air. Cold sweat ran off of us onto the vinyl seats as we kissed and our limbs wriggled around uncomfortably. In our underwear, I kept floating in and out of consciousness. Suddenly Asher stopped.

"What is it?" I slurred sloppily.

"You're too drunk. I'm taking you home," he said in a matter of fact tone as he pulled his pants back on.

I sat there for a moment, in my G-string, disappointed and confused.

"But I want to," I whined.

"Me too," Asher laughed. "We will, but not tonight, not like this. Get dressed."

I stumbled to get my clothing on, embarrassed, as my heart sank into my stomach. I had only ever been rejected once before.

~ ~ ~ ~ ~

When I was eighteen, I was completely in love with my best friend Sean, and had been for years. He was tall and skinny and his hair color changed from bright blue to bleach blond on a weekly basis. One night in university we were on the couch in his parents' basement after a night of clubbing with Baz Luhrmann's *Romeo + Juliet* playing in the background. I was wearing a low-cut top with ample cleavage and kept rubbing my leg up against Sean's. I was leaning and posing and pouting in the sexiest way I knew how (which in hindsight probably wasn't remotely sexy at all) and he wasn't paying any attention to me. During Mercutio's death scene, I turned to him and then looked away and then turned to him again and then looked away and then, finally, without looking at him. "I love you...I think I love you," I whispered, too embarrassed to face him.

"OH SHIT!" he gasped, then turned away and started sobbing. "I'm gay," he whispered painfully.

He came out of the closet to me right then and there...I know the whole obsession with Leo DiCaprio films should have tipped me off, but I was kinda slow when it came to stuff like that. Plus I was in love with the guy...

"I don't care, I love you. I want you to be my first," I screeched through my tears.

I forced myself on him and tried kissing him anyway. I climbed on top of him, wrestling with him, but he slid out from under me. We looked at one another and collapsed into each other's arms, sobbing and holding onto each other, fearing our friendship was over. He looked at me with sadness and compassion. He'd never given me any reason to think he was interested in me that way, but then again, he didn't do anything to make it clear he wasn't either. Then he told me about Chris, his boyfriend.

I was devastated; all our dreams of us taking Hollywood by storm together disintegrated. We were supposed to make movies together and have a mansion in The Hills and babies and live happily ever after doing cocaine with David Lynch and Oliver Stone. I was completely distraught...I was also proud of Sean for being brave enough to come out to me...even though I felt like he had this whole other life he'd been hiding from me. I also knew how hard it can be to come out, so I let it go of my own drama. I was touched I was the first one he told about his new life.

Like any good friend, I went clubbing with him the next night in the Gay-borhood to meet Chris and his new crew...Watching him with Chris wasn't easy for me, but it showed my solidarity.

Since that night with Sean, I'd never put myself in a position where I could be rejected again...

~ ~ ~ ~ ~

Asher's rejection made my stomach queasy, or maybe that was the alcohol. He called an Uber and kissed me goodnight.

The next morning, severely hungover, I was relieved that he was a decent guy and didn't take advantage of me in some drunken semi-conscious state.

Three days went by and I still hadn't heard from Asher. My insides were in turmoil waiting for the phone to ring, and my vagina had been on fire for days. I wasn't even really into him, but the rejection did not sit well with me, nor did the female version of blue balls, if there is a term for it.

I didn't know what to do with myself when masturbation didn't work so I wrote about all the confusing feelings I had and I ended up writing my first erotic poem. I have no idea where it came from but it poured out of me.

DRUNK IN THE CARGO VAN

Laid flat
On my back
In the back
Behind a shack
Experiencing a severe lack
In judgment...

Sitting, waiting, anticipating
Almost hating what's to come

Dirty pleasure makes love ugly
And sin snuggly against my skin

A sudden stop
My heart drops
My thoughts rock
Nipples pop erect

Cold sweat
Wet lips
Juice drips between my legs
My loneliness begs for attention

Everyone looks, but no one sees
Beyond a body, a tortured soul
Losing control
Desperately clinging
In my mind singing
Telephone not ringing...

Kelly reassured me Asher would call and, if he didn't, there were plenty of other fish in the city. "You are beautiful and fabulous and any man who wouldn't want you is a fool!" she declared.

I wanted to believe her, but I was still so insecure around guys, because I didn't look like Beth. When would I ever shake that? Inside I knew I was so much more than what people could see on the outside. All I could do was imagine Beth on the cover of a *Maxim*-type magazine, glistening, with her nipples protruding through a drenched white wife beater. For some reason, I felt like if I wasn't that, guys wouldn't ever really be interested in me. Even though Trevor and Asher worked against that theory, I had trouble believing it. I couldn't figure out why I was so down on myself at the time, but in retrospect I blame the media. It is totally the negative reinforcement of the media that made me so insecure as a girl and a young woman. Almost every single commercial, magazine, and billboard I came across reinforced what I didn't live up to.

On Saturday, Asher finally texted me, six days later. He invited me to a crazy loft party in Bushwick, Brooklyn, but I already had plans with Kelly to go to Ricky's Fashion Show. Every year, Ricky's leather boutique threw a huge benefit the weekend closest to Valentine's Day, a fetish fashion show to raise money for AIDS awareness and at-risk LGBTQ youth. It was literally the craziest party of the year and I was looking forward to a fun night out. I texted Asher that I already had plans. He texted back to come after...

~ ~ ~ ~ ~

I was a horny twenty-year-old virgin, on my own for the first time in New York City, when I met Ricky. My parents totally flipped out when I told them I was moving to New York after university. My mom insisted the only way she would let me go alone to New York was if I stayed with Ricky, my Aunt Rita's nephew. She insisted I would be safe with him because he was Jewish and Canadian and gay. So I lived with Ricky for two months while I got acclimated with the city, until I moved in with Kelly.

Ricky lived in a loft on Prince Street, a block away from the Angelika art house theater, both East and West villages right in the heart of SoHo—literally in the center of it all. Ricky was super cool and in his mid-thirties—a slim, playful guy with brown hair in an edgy coif and hazel eyes usually highlighted by some shimmer shadow. I'd often catch him admiring his butt in the mirror, and there were mirrors all over the place. I thought he was totally vain at first, but eventually clued in that they were clearly for Ricky to watch while having sex.

Ricky was always in a good mood, the total life of the party, and hilarious with his over-the-top dramatic reactions. He was a designer for a leather store where they sold pants, jackets, skirts, dresses, ball gags, crotchless chaps, riding crops, latex body suits and bondage accoutrements...items I was foreign to when I arrived.

Steve, Ricky's man, was a little skinnier than Ricky (but no one ever talked about that) and more on the intellectual side. He had ash blond hair, soft blue eyes, and the whole preppy thing going on. Steve was an editor at an online political mag and pretty much lived at

Ricky's place. They both sat on my bed in my room asking the basic 'getting to know you' questions as I unpacked.

"So Dana, it's your first night on your own in New York City. You gonna go find some hottie and get laid?" Ricky grinned mischievously.

I giggled nervously, almost embarrassed. "I'm saving myself Ricky, for *the one*," I confessed quietly.

Ricky thought it was cute that I was still a virgin, but was constantly trying to impart his philosophy of promiscuity on me.

"A virgin? You're serious? Girl! Don't listen to what your parents or Republicans tell you about sex. It's not bad or wrong or dirty. It is literally the driving force of the universe. Think about it…how the fuck did we all get here?"

He paused for me to process the question.

"Yeah! And what will happen if, all of a sudden, we all stop fuck-ing—right? The human race ceases to exist. It's the most natural thing in the world, and gay sex ensures population control. Just use a condom, baby," Ricky preached as he flailed his body around the room making a dramatic point.

"Now, gangbangs on the other hand, there is nothing natural there…but don't discount them, they are a hell of a fun night. That's how Steve and I met. My last boyfriend threw me a gangbang for my thirtieth birthday. I met Steve there, we split a hit of X and we've been together ever since. Best birthday I ever had." Ricky made his way over to Steve, who was now sitting on the couch in my room, and kissed him affectionately.

My eyes almost popped out of my head. Gangbangs? TMI. And Ewwww!

"Just use a condom, and I hate to burst your bubble, baby, but there isn't just one *the one*," he concluded. Then he shot Steve a look and they both got serious. Steve took over.

"Dana, since we'll all be living together for the next while, there is something you need to know."

"Okay." I was a little nervous. Would they be having gangbangs here on Tuesdays?

"Both Ricky and I are HIV positive."

My heart dropped, I had so many questions but bit my tongue, not knowing if any were appropriate. Were they dying?

"We are fine," Steve continued. "They have great treatments now. It's not a death sentence, and you can't contract it from living with us or having dinner together or even from sharing a joint. It is only transmitted through blood or sperm, not saliva."

I nodded, not sure what to say.

"You just need to know in case there is an accident or something," Ricky added.

I'd been in New York for less than an hour and it was clear I was no longer in a sheltered suburbia of carpools and private schools.

Ricky jumped up, "Okay, now that that's over, let's go for some Thai food? Our treat!"

And that was that.

Ricky and Steve took me on as their project, determined to break down my walls of prude-ness; they would tear my bathrobe from me, insisting I walk around naked, that I would feel more inspired and creatively charged (which I did) and that they were gay and weren't impressed by my perky tits. They pushed me to spend more time on my hair and makeup, dictated what I wore and what I ate. It was like I was in some alternate universe where I was encouraged to experiment and express myself, basically the opposite of living at home, with parents.

~ ~ ~ ~ ~

Saturday nights you could always expect a show in the subway: a mariachi band, two dance troupes, and one kid selling chocolates for his basketball team later, we arrived at the Lorimer stop in Williamsburg. We walked almost twenty minutes through what seemed like an abandoned industrial part of Brooklyn before we got to the warehouse where the party was being held.

Kelly and I wandered deeper into the unknown streets of Brooklyn, searching for the party. The area was so desolate and run down. Finally, we rounded a corner and were greeted by a gust of wind charging toward us coming right off of the East River. It was frigid, but the beauty of the lights from the city glistening off the water made the cold bearable. We could see our breath in the frosty night air. As we walked closer to the water, we could hear music bumping and the sounds of drunken laughter.

Kelly and I entered a suspicious-looking warehouse by the water and walked into a scene out of Andy Warhol's factory. Lights flashing, avant-garde experimental films screening on the walls, body painting in one corner, techno spinning from the rafters, and a catwalk extending out from a large stage. The cross section of a funky, diverse New York crowd included everything from bankers to Drag Queens. "Anything goes at the fetish show." That was literally their slogan.

Ricky was backstage wrangling his crew of models, stylists, and hair and makeup artists, approving finishing touches, the order, the music, and final lighting cues. The place was packed to capacity and everyone was excited to be there. The entire room went dark, then silent. Showtime. Lights came up on a fog-filled stage with a group of models draped in togas, frozen in a tableau of a Dionysian Greek orgy scene in provocative positions. Every member of the LGBTQ community was represented on stage from ethnic diversity to orientation. After a long pause, the DJ pumped up the beats, and the models shed their sheets and started to strut their stuff down the catwalk. The outfits and actions grew raunchier and more risqué as the show went on, each trying to top the previous scene. There were bondage demonstrations, spanking sessions, and a voguing contest to end the show. The crowd went wild for the spectacle and erupted into a dance party.

Once everything post-show was under control, Ricky and his man Steve found us on the dance floor. Ricky gave me a quick hug as I raved about his fabulosity, then he disappeared into the crowd of his gushing fans. Steve stayed to dance with us. He was grinding Kelly and they both took off their shirts. Kelly had little need for a bra so she rarely wore one, sporting black pasties over her nipples. It was hot with all the sweaty bodies dancing and wriggling against each other.

I hadn't been out dancing since before the breakup; I'd forgotten how much I loved it, how freeing the sensation was, and I surrendered. My hair whipped across my face as moisture collected on my forehead and down my neck. I continued swinging my body as I brushed my hair out of my face and wiped the sweat away. The song ended and I walked away from the dance floor, catching my breath. I felt free and feverish, like an animal on the prowl, and foolish at the same time for wasting nearly a year of my life pining over a memory. It was time for action, time for fun, time to get wild!

I felt eyes on me, as sweat ran down my back. The room, the world, was full of guys; all I had to do was wake up and notice them. In line for the bathroom I met a Columbian journalist with dark skin and penetrating eyes. He placed half a hit of an MDMA pill in my hand. I slowly put it on my tongue and swallowed it.

"You're so sexy; I've never seen anyone move like that." He leaned in to press his lips against mine.

He kissed me in a way that made me feel so alone. His desire to consume me was frightening. I was afraid because I could have easily given into him, and left with him right then and there and let him destroy me over and over again. I wasn't ready for that yet. I needed to ease back into the game. The journalist let me go ahead of him in line and kissed my hand as I disappeared behind the bathroom door. I intentionally lost him after my turn in the loo. He was coming on way too strong.

I was pushing my way through bouncing hips and flailing arms to find Kelly, when I saw this fairylike creature twinkling out of the corner of my eye. She was spinning around on the dance floor with her green glitter eye shadow sparkling in the crowd. She looked over at me and motioned for me to join her. Entranced, I went. She took my hands in hers and smiled at me with her Rhianna smile. She had smooth tan skin, was rocking a Mohawk, and wore a leather corset and angel wings. The ecstasy I totally forgot I had taken kicked in and her hands felt like silk against mine. As the drug washed over me, I surrendered to her trance. It could have been minutes or days there with her on the dance floor. She grabbed me and kissed me. Her lips tasted like cotton candy as they melted in my mouth.

"Let's get some drinks, you got me sweatin'," she shouted over the music as her hand ran down my arm, taking mine and leading me to the bar. "I'm Kymia," she said in a Trinidadian accent. I nodded my head. She continued talking, but I had no idea what she was saying, something about doing a master's degree at Rutgers. I couldn't really hear anything, I could just feel sounds moving through my body as I stared at her perfectly shaped lips, eyes and nose.

After hydrating, Kym and I went back on the dance floor for a few more songs. Steve and Ricky were dancing next to us and Kelly was fooling around in a corner with a new female friend. We had all somehow managed to be separately and secretly rolling on MDMA. Each of us happened upon it in our own way, not seeking it out, just being discreetly offered and each of us accepting.

It was past one a.m. when Kelly and her lady took off and I was left alone with Kym on the dance floor. I pulled out my phone to check the time. I had three missed calls from Asher. I went into the hallway to check my messages. I didn't notice Kym behind me until I was already listening to Asher's voice on the other end. I pulled the phone away from my ear and said, "It's just…"

"Some guy," she interrupted. "Some guy you really like…"

I didn't know if I really liked Asher, but I knew I wanted him to like me and I was horny as hell. We had already gotten pretty close to naked together, and I knew him, so it wasn't like fucking a random.

"He wants you to come see him, yeah?" she asked.

I nodded.

"There's this hipster party with live music in Bushwick," I said. "It's supposed to be pretty fun. Wanna come with?"

She nodded.

The Bushwick party was a totally different BoHo/Hipster scene. There were kegs of beer and the whole place reeked of weed. There had been a few bands but it was almost two a.m. by the time we arrived, so the live music was over. Asher introduced Kym and me to a few of his friends and we all found ourselves on the dance floor. Kym and I couldn't stand still; the drugs were still running through our veins and keeping the body moving was essential to prevent the brain from sensory overload.

My body kept falling and flailing between Kym and Asher on the dance floor, my lips on hers, his hands on my waist, grinding his pelvis on my ass, his lips against my neck as my fingertips danced across Kym's thin body. I turned around and leaned in to kiss Asher. He kissed me for a few seconds and then Kym pulled me away and I fell onto her lips. This tug of war dance continued for a few moments as my body flip-flopped between the two of them. Eventually, Asher pulled away and went down the hall. I followed him, leaving Kym twirling around under the flashing blue and red lights.

He got himself a beer. I searched for a bottle of water and settled for a Coke.

"Hey," I said to Asher while stumbling over into him. "Cool party."

He just nodded his head. "Who's your friend?" he asked suspiciously.

"Kym? I…uh…just met her, at that ah…other…party. Isn't she cool?" I said in a disoriented drugged-out state. I grabbed his collar and pulled his lips into mine, kissing him hard.

"Do you want to have a threesome with her? Is that why you brought her?"

I was in total shock. "What are you talking about?" I began laughing! "Threesome? I'm not into girls!"

"Are you sure?" he asked me with a smile on his face. "Because it seems like you are, or at least you're into her."

He had a point. I was going two for two making out with girls while hanging out with Asher.

"I think you're still mixed up from your breakup," he told me in a tone way too serious for three on a Sunday morning. "I think you are a little damaged coming out of that relationship and decided you have some figuring out to do." He gave me a sympathetic hug. "I'm calling you an Uber. If you're not going home with her, make sure she gets there safely. You seem reckless right now, and, frankly, I'm worried about you."

Me, reckless? Not even close! But I was confused. I wasn't into women. Was this somehow a subconscious way of protecting myself so I didn't hook up with the wrong guy?

Maybe it was time to actually *get* reckless, to get out there and have more fun nights like that. Maybe not a full on raunchy one-night stand or a threesome, but to be more open to possibility. I had years of lost time to make up for and needed to cut through my own bullshit. The past two months had been terrible teases. Let's face it, my vagina was frustrated.

CYBERSLUT

"Do I mind if Doug joins in?" I froze, wearing nothing but a periwinkle lace thong.

TIME OUT!

This was wrong on so many levels I didn't even know where to begin; first of all, none of us were on ecstasy. Second of all, what if I *did* mind? And finally, wasn't this kinda gay?

I mean, I know I'd only been with one guy, but weren't they all about being with two girls, four girls, seventy-two virgins...I'd never heard of a guy stop in the middle and say, "Hey babe, mind if my buddy gets in on this?"

As my sexual needs reached a boiling point it occurred to me that I really needed to cum and couldn't hold out for Mr. Right any longer. And I don't mean like shaving your legs or flossing kinda cum, just to take care of business—I mean full-body eruption kind of orgasm where every cell in your body is tingling, the kind you need a partner for.

"Where does a woman in Manhattan go to find a man to sweep her off her feet and make her his princess?" I groaned at Kelly.

"*Princess?* Have you looked out the window? Life is no fairytale; there is no enchanted forest out there and no Prince Charming coming to your rescue. You have to save yourself!"

"I lived in a basement in Queens for three years! It's time I felt like fucking royalty!"

"You are hysterical, Dana. If you don't have sex soon, I'm gonna do you with my strap on, I swear."

"Hysterical? Aren't you exaggerating just a little?" I huffed.

"No, I'm being scientifically accurate. Look it up," she retorted snarkily. "Hysteria. It's a medical term from the Victorian era when women weren't *allowed* to have sexual desires. Women would get so horny they would go crazy and have to go to the doctor a few times a week to be relieved by clitoral stimulation."

"Are you joking? I really can't tell."

"It was such an epidemic, it's how the vibrator got invented. By a doctor whose hand got too sore and tired from rubbing pussy all day."

I quickly referred to Wikipedia, and, to my disbelief, Kelly's story held up. Women go hysterical when they get sexually frustrated. Who knew? This was something they definitely left out of sex ed in middle school.

It dawned on me, sex isn't remotely as special as a girl's mother tells her when gently explaining the birds and the bees, but females are the ones who end up pregnant. Sex is a biological function used against women to control us. Men were never repressed to the point of having a medical condition for their blue balls. No one criticizes men for having fun and exploring themselves, but promiscuous women are often shunned and shamed…Why is a family's honor hinged on their daughter's sexual activity? But not their son's? Because men can shoot a load and run with no evidence of the act; women are the ones left with the repercussions, with the decisions, with the pro-lifers violently protesting them for making smart decisions and not messing up more kids' lives by bringing them into the world when they are not in a position to care for them properly, as if there aren't enough neglected children already.

My fantasy world notions of true love crumbled around me. All that was left was the harsh, concrete reality of Hell's Kitchen.

I wasn't keen on the cyber-dating thing to begin with; chemistry is hard to gauge via a screen, but, after what happened with Asher, and a push from both Kelly and Ricky, I decided to give it a shot.

The trouble was I had been settled down for four years with Russell; part of me wanted adventure and the other part still wanted to find *the one.* Could I possibly find both in the same guy? I turned to cyber dating for some answers. I carefully worded my profile and answered the questions provided, checking off my hobbies, favorite foods and activities. Kelly took a few fresh pics, then we jumped into the cyber abyss.

At first, I was excited to browse through all the eligible men who were looking for their other half. I was inundated with instant messages and matches; it was hard to keep up with all the guys who suddenly wanted to know me. I was careful with my selections of who to respond to. I made sure they were cute and had at least a master's degree. I was going for the opposite of Russell—someone practical—so hot, college dropouts were not being considered.

The first one was a chef. He had less hair than in his picture, his hairline was receding considerably, and he was three or four inches shorter than his profile stated. Rule #1 of dating apps: men lie about their height and their hair (women lie about their weight and their age). He was well-dressed in a generic, lacking-style kind of way. We met at a trendy place in the East Village and he tried to order for me so we could share a few dishes. A nice gesture, but he didn't ask what I liked or if I was a vegetarian (who sometimes ate fish) so when he finished telling the waitress what I was going to have, I changed my order. He wasn't pleased. How considerate. But it had literally been years since I'd been on a date and I was rusty, so I stayed.

We sipped our drinks as we waited for the food. He talked about where he grew up in Michigan and his boring job. Well, maybe his job wasn't so boring, maybe it was just him. He asked me about my job. I didn't say much. I didn't know what I was doing there. When the dessert menus came, I lied and told him I was having really bad period cramps and had to go lie down. I excused myself before the check came and headed home.

Over a pint of mint chocolate cookie ice cream Kelly reassured me, "You are going to have to go through some frogs before you find your fish. Don't let one bad date get to you. Just pick out another one."

So I did.

The second one had all his hair. He was also a few inches shorter than his profile said, but at least he was attractive. He had light brown hair and brown eyes, and was dressed very well in a suit, tie, and shiny, new shoes. This one was a graphic designer born and raised in the UK and boy was he charming. I loved his British accent. He took me to a Broadway Show starring Matthew Broderick and it was delightful. I was impressed that he went to see theater, since it was totally my thing. Afterward, we grabbed a late dinner at a delicious Brazilian place on restaurant row. A hidden treasure in the middle of my neighborhood that I never knew about but just the kind I love. I was definitely feeling some sparks. It felt nice to be treated for a change. Maybe it was the show, or the great food, or maybe I had found a decent guy.

After dinner, we walked up Ninth Avenue and ended up near Lincoln Center. It was a mild night for March and the walk was refreshing after the wine. He led me to the door of a building and invited me in.

"You live here?" I asked surprised by the swanky digs.

"My parents do," he said with a smile.

"You live with your parents?"

He started laughing. "God no, I'm in the West Village and they're out of town. They have a better view and I have the key."

I followed him up to the penthouse overlooking Lincoln Center. The apartment was impeccably decorated with a mix of pop and classical art. The lavish hardwood floor and granite countertops reminded me of something out of a magazine. He led me into a sitting room and opened a bottle of wine from the bar, poured two glasses and handed me one. We sat on the couch and sipped the wine as we giggled and snuggled in closer to each other. His lips brushed against mine and we started kissing. It felt nice.

"You have to come see the view," he whispered in my ear.

He led me up a tight spiral staircase that led to the roof. The view was spectacular and I could see the Hudson River on one side and Central Park on the other. I didn't even notice the rooftop hot tub until he turned the jets on. "Are you up for some relaxation?"

I got nervous. I wasn't prepared to disrobe just yet. "I have to go home, I have to work early," I apologized.

"Stay, I'll make you breakfast. My parents get back in a couple of days so I don't know when we will have this opportunity again."

I politely declined. I found my jacket, scarf, gloves and wrapped myself up. He insisted on walking me down and putting me in an Uber. I was impressed by his manners, his taste in restaurants, the fact he was a patron of the arts; however, I was not impressed that he tried to get me naked in a hot tub on the first date. It's unfortunate because I would have loved to hang out on a rooftop hot tub surrounded by the lights of the city with him. Why couldn't he have been more patient? Or at least given me warning to bring a swimsuit?

"Why couldn't you have been more fun? Why is the problem with him? He sounds great! The show, the dinner, the hot tub, everything!" Kelly scolded me for not seizing the opportunity to have a sexy night in a rooftop hot tub overlooking the city with a guy I was, in fact, into.

"You're the one who messed up that date. If you were into him you should have just gone with the moment. Come on, Dana, I thought we discussed this. From now on you have a new rule. When in fabulous situations like the one tonight I want you to ask yourself, 'What Would Kelly Do?' Then do that instead of what you would do. #WWKD!" she smirked, proud of her revelation.

"Oy vey," I sighed; this wasn't a challenge I was up for.

"You could have left your bra and undies on and carried the wet garments home in a plastic bag. You could have made out and fooled around a bit; not all guys expect to have sex on a first date—guess what, most don't! Think about it, most relationships these days begin with hooking up on the first date…if the chemistry is there and the moment feels right, life is too short not to experience it. I'm sorry, if I'm not mistaken, didn't Russell spend the night in your bed before you even went on your first date?"

She had me there. Point made. New Rule: What Would Kelly Do? #WWKD?

I let Kelly pick the next guy. At least I could blame her next time things went wrong.

Jonathan was a doctor from the Upper East Side, training to be a surgeon. He was a country club type of guy with blond hair and brown eyes. He had a firm, husky body and a sweet smile. He was intelligent, polite and paid the check…there was no doubt that this guy was a prize.

My mind was racing since our eyes first met. He was great on paper and in person. Someone my mother would love as much as I could. The first date was nice, dinner in Little Italy, fun, casual. The second was a movie, and he held my hand. We had fun together; he gave me a book, he brought me home to his parents, offered to take me shopping. In less than two weeks we had gone on five dates, but by the third date I realized something was off…and by the fifth still no tongue. I needed to call an expert for backup.

"Five dates, no tongue?" Ricky shouted into the phone. "You went out on five different occasions and not once did he try to put his tongue in your mouth?"

"Yes," I confirmed.

"He offered to take you shopping, but never tried to tap your shit?"

"Yup."

"Girl, what kind of guy would rather go shopping than hook up?"

Kelly and Ricky both confirmed my suspicion, or paranoia: he must be gay! But maybe he wasn't ready to admit that yet. I was really disappointed. Jonathan was the first glimmer of light. I let him down easy and wished him well. I had a history of being attracted to gay guys and being completely clueless to the signs. Ever since the incident with Sean in university I couldn't help but be overly suspicious.

It had been a month of cyberdating and my trial membership was a few days away from expiring. I made the decision not to renew. In three and a half weeks I had two bad dates and a mini-relationship with no tongue.

It was the last week of March, on a Wednesday night, when I had my last 'chat.' This hot investment banker in his thirties started messaging me. David. We made plans for Friday night. He was dressed in an Armani suit and looked impeccable, like out of a movie, but better. I was wearing a simple short black dress and killer heels. His smell was intoxicating, but not overpowering, in a fresh ocean breeze kind of way.

He took me to Bouley, one of the fanciest restaurants in town. I was impressed that he took me somewhere so extravagant on a first date. It was decadent, from the food to the décor. We were seated at a banquet in the corner. The lights were dim. He ran his hand up my leg under the crisp white tablecloth as he leaned into me and tickled my neck with his warm breath.

I was extremely attracted to this guy and aroused all through dinner. He kept his hand under the tablecloth the entire evening, exploring my legs, my calves, my knees, my thighs at his will. I didn't stop him like I usually would, but embraced the new rule of #WWKD. I enjoyed the tease. Truly, I missed being touched. He wandered too far with his hands more than once, his fingers at the edges of my panties while the server leaned across the table to remove my plate, but I remained silent. I had never played that game before, and Kelly was right, I was missing out on a lot of excitement.

We took our time with desert, feeding each other and looking into each other's eyes. We didn't talk much during the meal. I let out a tiny gasp as his hands explored under the table, mostly our bodies did the talking.

By the end of the date I was horny as hell. Why not go home with this guy? He was the hottest guy who'd ever wanted me, other than Trevor. He must have dropped at least $300 on dinner and a bottle of champagne, which kept me swirling in his touch. He made me feel like a princess and I was ready to pounce.

This was totally the type of guy I could see myself with, so when he asked me to go back to his place, I went. Something Kelly said a few weeks back resonated. Every relationship she had started out with hooking up on the first date. That's just how things were now. Even with Russell, the chemistry was hard to fight against. He slept over our first night together. Was she right? There was only one way to find out. #WWKD?

We took a cab back to his place, in lower Manhattan. We made out sensuously in the taxi. His hands were up my dress and he was trying to expose my panties in the back seat. I could see the cab driver's eyes glancing in the rearview mirror in curiosity, trying to see what he was missing. David paid the driver and we went up to his condo.

In the elevator, he explained that he owned the place and let his buddy Doug rent the second bedroom. The place had a sleek modern design. Something I would imagine a young successful banker to live in downtown. David opened another bottle of bubbles and we sat down on the couch. As we sipped, Doug, the roommate appeared. David introduced us and offered him a glass. Doug declined, chatted with us a few moments then excused himself. David had his hand on my left leg the entire time, inching it higher and higher up my thigh.

"Would you like to see the view from my room?" he asked in a seductive tone. This time I understood what he meant by *view*. I hesitantly followed him into his bedroom. I was shocked how easy it was for me. I closed the door behind me, let him unzip my dress, and was standing at the edge of his bed in my lace G-string, push-up bra and heels.

He hung up his jacket as he watched me, studying my body as I stood there. He unbuttoned his shirt, placed his cufflinks in the drawer and unbuckled his belt. He caressed my shoulders and ran his hands over my ass, then spanked me. It stung, I gasped. He kissed my mouth and brushed my hair away from my face. He ran his fingertips along my lips and pushed two fingers into my mouth, staring deep into my eyes. He took his fingers out of my mouth and pushed me back onto the bed. He slid his pants off and tossed them over a chair, then climbed on top of me, licking up my leg.

I wriggled my body underneath him as he licked his way up to my stomach. He took off my bra, and sucked each nipple tenderly, giving equal attention to each one. He grabbed my legs behind my knees and pushed back, spreading my legs wide, angling my pelvis towards the ceiling. He licked up each thigh and then opened his mouth onto the material separating him from my treasure. The material dampened as he exhaled hot air onto my panties, his mouth covering my barely hidden pussy. He licked the outside of my panties as he pulled down his boxers exposing his very impressive sidekick. I took him in my hands and stroked gently, hoping I hadn't lost any of my skills in the past year of celibacy. I kept stroking him.

I turned my head to the side, preparing to take him in my mouth, and noticed Doug leaning in the doorway watching, wearing a towel and gliding his hand over where the material was beginning to tent. The towel fell to the floor, and he stroked his larger than average enthusiasm as he came toward the bed. Apparently, I wasn't the only one invited to the party.

David smiled and assured me that it was okay. "I'm cool with it; you don't mind if Doug joins in, do you?"

I froze.

It was the attack of the monster cocks! They were both huge and frightening as a pair. I have to admit I did, for a second, consider it. Come on, men aren't the only ones who think double the tongues, double the fun. And what about my new rule, #WWKD? I can't speak for other women, but hell yeah, I'd fantasized about being with two men. Four strong hands, two sets of wet lips, two big, beautiful...and then it occurred to me...sure, the fantasy is that I would be the queen ordering my slave boys around, directing them where to go and when to pick up the pace, but, who was I kidding? Sex was never like that for me with one guy. What are the chances it would be like that with two? I had a flash of a stiff jaw and a mild case of whiplash. Sorry Kelly, this one was way over my head.

I gathered my things and was out the door. The two of them sat naked, staring at each other in disbelief.

"Have you learned nothing from me at all? What about our new hashtag?" Kelly scolded. "I have dreamed of that opportunity my entire life, and you just turned it down! I thought you were looking for fun and excitement and adventure..."

"I want to be with someone where there is a possibility of a future. A guy who wants to share and watch me with his friend, first of all, can't be looking for something serious, second, is a little too adventurous for me; I'm not that open minded. And, third, is probably kinda gay, or at least bi, right?"

"It's a damn shame, a damn shame, girl. What I would have done to those boys..." Kelly trailed off, as she got lost in a daydream.

The next day my trial membership on the dating app had officially expired, so I decided to give it a rest and try meeting someone the old-fashioned way; like at Starbucks or yoga or something.

APR | DIRTY, SEXY, AWESOMENESS

"Devour me? Wait a second!?" I moaned, trying to come up for air.

"You're right." Tony pulled himself off of me. "I'm sorry. I've been hard the whole time on the train, I've been so excited to see you." He grabbed his crotch, readjusting his erection in his jeans. "I just wanted to see if you were wet, waiting."

My hysteria hit a breaking point as Kelly's latest romance was heating up. Drew, a skinny, freckly redhead with a bunch of tats, a hipster beard and topknot, was a PhD student in Afro-Musicology at NYU when he was sober enough to make it to class. The rest of the time he lived in squalor in a crawl space in Brooklyn with the rest of his band, a bunch of trust fund brats from Connecticut posing as starving artists, but secretly spending small fortunes on their alternative lifestyle of grass-fed beef, organic pressed juice and craft beers.

I didn't get their music or why Kelly was stuck on musicians after all the heartache I went through with Russell, but he was pleasant and a little shy and good for her. She took his virginity years back, her first week of school freshman year at NYU. Back then he was totally intimidated by her, but now he could almost handle her. He was a wacky creative with a high IQ like her, so it's no surprise they stimulated one another.

The most annoying thing about their relationship was listening to them have sex constantly. It was driving me crazy, because I needed it so bad. Don't get me wrong, I was totally happy for them, but it was getting obnoxious; they were doing it morning, midday, and all through the night. He had a dick that just wouldn't quit. I was in awe of how long they could go at it. Wasn't he afraid his penis would break? And wasn't she sore?

The city was thawing out from the winter when Kelly gave me a gift certificate to see Yara. Kelly and I had been going to Yara's for years. That's where I took Kelly for her first facial. Soon after she started bikini waxing there too, which became a bi-monthly ritual for her, especially in her line of work. Kelly didn't work naked, but her outfits were beyond risqué. Yara was an eccentric Russian woman who was pushing sixty, but dressed like she was twenty. She was tall and skinny, with a pronounced pouch of a gut that hung over her two-sizes-too-small studded low rider jeans. She wore too much makeup and even more perfume to cover up the cigarette smell, but she gave the best facial in town. Her husband left her before she made it to America and she busted her ass putting her daughter through Princeton and taking care of her elderly mother.

I buzzed the buzzer and she came strolling to the door. The salon was small and cramped. The foyer was cluttered with gaudy hair accessories, bejeweled yoga wear, and knockoff designer handbags for sale. There were some autographed pictures on the walls from some of her quasi-celebrity clients and a few framed magazine articles where her salon was mentioned.

"Challo shvettie," she greeted me with her thick Russian accent and raspy voice as she gave me a hug. "You chave new boyfriend yet?" she asked.

I shook my head, no. All I needed was for her to rub it in. She began to lecture me.

"You know your problem, you're too picky. Just pick vone vith good job from good family and marry him. Zat's it, not so chard. You American, ay I sorry, Canadian vhatever, you so silly. You listen from me...Love is bullshit. Zere is no love. Zere is chard life and chard vork or easy life vith rich man if he's not asshole. But zey all asshole. So how much ve vaxings today?" she asked.

"Eyebrow and bikini," I said, presenting the gift certificate from Kelly.

"Kelly is crazy," she muttered as she shook her head.

I could just imagine Kelly naked, spread eagle on Yara's table, describing her last dominatrix session with a Hassidic man who liked to be spanked with a studded paddle.

"Kelly said me tell you zat certificate is to do Brazilian vax, you no chave to, but come on, chave some funs," she said with a wide smile.

Fun for whom? Hot wax on the edge of my pussy lips tearing out hair is only fun for one person: the man who gets to enjoy the pussy lips, and I had a vacancy in my pussy-lip-enjoyment department, so it seemed like a waste...or an invitation for the universe to fill that vacancy...

I have this theory: Sometimes you can't change the big things in life but you can make small little changes that might trigger the bigger changes. Like a different color nail polish, a haircut, removal of all my pubic hair...so what the hell.

"Take off panties, lie on stomach and chold open cheeks...you vill love, I promise."

Can you believe that ten years ago women actually had hair on their vaginas? Now, it's pretty much taboo. I took off my panties, lay on my stomach, spread open my ass cheeks and let out a shriek as she tore a strip of wax from my crack...

When I got home, I took a long hot shower to remove the excess wax and pry my cheeks apart. I followed by slathering lotion all over my body and wrapping up in a fluffy blue robe and fuzzy slippers. Curious, I sat on my bed and examined my bare nether regions with a mirror. As I lay back, I was contemplating whether to make plans for the night or stay in and masturbate. Kelly bought me a Rabbit for Christmas and it was still sitting in the drawer unused...Then all of the sudden my phone rang. I was startled. I jerked myself up, embarrassed, and answered it.

"Hello."

"How you doin', Dana?" the voice on the other end inquired in a thick Brooklyn Italian accent a la Joey Tribbiani.

"Tony?" my voice went up in excitement.

"What's up beautiful? Guess who's in town?"

My heart began to race. "For real?"

"That's right, baby. I haven't stopped thinking about you in a million years. How ya been?"

I guess the universe listened to my Brazilian...

~ ~ ~ ~ ~

Tony and I were part of the same theater company before he took the plunge and moved to Hollywood. When Russell was gone on the road Tony was a friend to confide in and see plays with until he switched coasts. He was a hot, dark, Italian guy from Brooklyn, with cute dimples, green eyes, olive skin and a sensitive side, so I could really talk to him. A year ago, before he left town, I went to his place to say goodbye after sharing a pizza at his favorite spot in Brooklyn. We were sitting on his couch smoking some weed when I took a notebook out from my bag.

"I wrote something. I was thinking of doing it at the Monday night Open Mic. Can I read it? I haven't shared it with anyone yet."

"Sure," he nodded.

I flipped through my notebook, found the page and proceeded to read aloud.

WONDERFUL DISASTER

You are for me the most wonderful disaster
The reason why I'll never have a happily ever after
I'm sitting here dreaming of the sweet hereafter
Unable to bare a world without the sound of your beautiful laughter

My heart is shaking
On the verge of breaking
While the earth around me is quaking
I can't tell if I'm asleep or waking

It hurts to breathe
I hate that I need (you)
If I were strong I would just leave
But before you I crumble
Submitting to my master
Unable to avoid you
My most wonderful disaster

He was silent for a long moment.

"You wrote that? It's good, like really good..." he replied in admiration.

"Thanks," I said blushing, not sure what to do.

His eyes were penetrating through me as he said, "Uhhh, you have to leave right now or I'm going to tear your clothes off."

I paused in silence, staring at him.

"I'm not kiddin'. You gotta go, or I can't be held responsible for what happens."

I started laughing. He couldn't be serious, could he? I looked at him and his eyes were fixated on me.

"You gotta go." He stared at me in a way I had never experienced before. He grabbed my notebook and tossed it behind the couch.

Shit! *He was serious.* He climbed on top of me, straddled my hips on the couch, but I slid out from between his legs onto the floor. As I crawled away he grabbed my leg and pulled me towards him. My jean skirt rode up high on my thighs, pink G-string exposed.

He rolled me over, grabbed my wrists and pinned me down on the ground as he straddled me again. I couldn't help but feel excited and, for a brief microsecond, I relished the feeling of his hard body on top of me, wanting me; it had been a long time since I had been touched like that. Remembering Russell, I broke free, pushed him off of me, grabbed my bag and ran to the door. He pushed me up against the wall; I could feel his excitement pressing against my ass as he gently kissed my neck. My legs were trembling, nipples erect, thoughts racing, breath panting, insides shaking.

"If I didn't have a boyfriend, things would be different," I breathlessly whispered and opened the front door and darted down the hall before I lost control.

He chased me down the hallway, pushed me up against the wall in the stairwell, his hand caressing the back of my left calf, knee, thigh; he made it up to the crease between my leg, then ran his fingers along the elastic band of my panties. Once again, I tore myself away from him. I said goodbye and wished him well with the move.

I spent the next half hour moist on the N train trying to collect myself. I knew things were going to change...Russell didn't arouse me as intensely as Tony did, or hadn't in a very long time. I missed that feeling—the excitement of being wanted. I was flustered when I got home.

"Pretty baby, I've missed you." Russell snuck up behind me, wrapped his arms around me as I closed the door, startled.

"What are you doing here? You scared me." I was trembling, half-frightened to find someone in the apartment unexpectedly, half-nervous he could read all the bad, bad thoughts about Tony racing through my head.

"It's been weeks. You feel so good."

I let my weight fall into his arms as I draped myself around him.

"Louis has strep. We cancelled a few gigs. We have a whole week this time before I have to leave again." He pulled me in, kissed me on the lips and led me to the couch. I followed and curled into his lap. I was still so turned on from Tony and my body was on fire. I leaned in and kissed his neck. He flinched.

"What's that smell?" he pushed me off of him. "Like cheap cologne?"

"It's nothing," I said nervously.

Russell grabbed me by the chin and started smelling me with a sinister look in his eye.

"Who was on you, was someone kissing you, your neck?" he accused.

"I was rehearsing a scene," I defended.

"Is that what they call it?" he pushed.

If girls were throwing themselves at Russell the way Tony came on to me, what were the chances of him saying no every time? My stomach was in knots. His suspicions about me made me more suspicious of him. When I confronted him about it, he was adamant that he would never betray me. I didn't believe him, especially after I had come so close to betraying him.

That was the last week I spent with Russell. Once he was back on the road our relationship unraveled through text fights until I finally ended it two months later.

~ ~ ~ ~ ~

Ever since the day Tony wrestled me to the ground in his apartment, he had become a regular guest in my masturbation fantasies. Even though we never did anything beyond rubbing our bodies together fully clothed, the thought of him being so aggressive excited me. I was thrilled he reached out.

Tony and I made plans for the night. Dinner in Little Italy and then a late flick at the Angelika; he had a small role in this independent film screening there. I rushed around the apartment tidying up. I blew my hair dry, put on some makeup and hunted for the perfect outfit, one that said sexy, but not slutty, a hard line for me to define. Six outfits later I was ready for my hot date. I was ready for some fun.

I had known Tony for years. He was my friend, so there were no expectations in terms of a relationship. I had already decided that after the movie he would come back to my place and we would fool around like crazy, but no sex. I didn't need to have sex with him. I wasn't going to rush into that. Tony was only in town for two weeks and I didn't want to get hung up over him. I wasn't sure I could separate sex and emotions yet, especially after my Russell relapse. But I was up for pretty much everything else.

There was a knock at my door around seven thirty. I took one final glance in the mirror, primped one last time and headed for the door to greet Tony. Midway to the door I realized I had left the unopened Rabbit lying on my bed, I dove back into my room and hid it in a drawer, then continued to the door. He was leaning against the doorframe in his black leather jacket.

"How you doin'?" he asked with a half-smile as he made his way inside.

"Hi Ton…"

That's as far as I got before his lips made it to my mouth. He led me to the couch, while kissing me and wrapping his arms around my back. Within thirty seconds he had me on the floor; his teeth scratched down the side of my neck and his left hand caressed the inside of my thigh.

I'd never dated much, with the exception of the recent handful of cyberdates. Dating always seemed like an old-fashioned thing my parents did. It's something of a lost art with my generation. A date used to be a guy would pick up a girl at her parents' house. He would arrive extremely well-groomed with flowers, chocolates, or some sort of gift in order to have better chances of making it through to the second round.

The second round was the interrogation, usually conducted by the father. This is where the father had the opportunity to scare all the horniness out of the date before the daughter was allowed to leave the house. Then the couple would proceed to some sort of activity: the movies, dancing, bowling. They would get some food. Then the guy would have her back at a suitable time before his kneecaps were broken. If he was lucky and the dad wasn't spying on them, he might get a peck on the cheek.

Right away when the parents are taken out of the equation, the rules change. Now your date is actually thinking about you during the date. All the terrible things he wants to do to you, rather than having a bad case of shrinkage from the icy looks your father was giving him an hour earlier.

Most of my dating life took place after I moved out of my parents' house and was living on my own. This was bad. What a man and woman need while courting are many obstacles standing between them so they have this deep longing to be alone. Parents are a great obstacle. Living on one's own they're not in the way. This may seem like a good thing, but it actually ruins the entire dating ritual. Now, my date could enter a secluded space alone with me before we even went out on said date. And if you are attracted to your date this becomes a very dangerous situation.

It started off normal enough; boy asked girl out. Boy picked up girl. Girl looked hot, so did boy. Then things took a terrible turn, or not so terrible, depending on what angle you're watching from. You end up naked on the floor before you even leave for dinner. There were no obstacles, no boundaries, and look what happened. Even my relationship with Russell began with him spending the night in my bed before he ever took me out on a date. Maybe it's the initial raw attraction that determines if a man is relationship material, not the type of restaurant he takes you to.

The difference between my parents' generation and mine is that their relationships started with dating in order to get to the sex. Ours now start with sex in order to get to what?

My ideas of love and sex changed drastically once I learned about hysteria and acknowledged my biological/scientific need for sexual satisfaction independent of a loving (committed) relationship. This was hard to wrap my head around considering it went against everything I had been taught from such a young age.

Tony and I never made it out that night. Against my better judgment, we had sex on my floor, in my bed, and even in the shower, then still had time to Netflix and chill after. It was incredible. Nothing like with Russell at all. Tony was primal in his desire; he had a hunger that couldn't be satisfied, his mouth was eager, and he crossed invisible borders on my flesh that had never been explored as he bent me over, confusing my emotions in sheer dirty pleasure. I couldn't believe how well he knew his way around my body without ever having been there before. Good thing he came equipped with a box of condoms hidden in his jacket, because I was not prepared.

I had no expectations with Tony, so there was no pressure. I didn't care if he loved me, or even really liked me, so it was easy to let go. I just wanted to feel good physically. With his insatiable touch and sweet-talking, I lost all control and surrendered to the sensation of his tongue gliding up my skin, his fingers running down my body, and his excitement penetrating my quivering insides. He released the animal in me, and all my rules fell away into the ether…well all but one…#WWKD!

He spent the night and found his way inside me before my eyes were even open the next morning. I was already wet with anticipation as he slid between my legs while spooning me. We went for brunch to a trendy spot in SoHo, then caught the matinee screening of the flick he was in at the Angelika. We parted ways mid-afternoon, but he was back at my place in time to take me to a late dinner followed by another night of dirty, awesome, sexiness.

Tony devoured me several times, several ways, over several different days. We had a great time, and then he headed back to California. As much as I was satisfied with my spring fling, I couldn't help beating myself up about having a one-night—fine—four-night stand. I totally set myself up for disaster; I was getting attached to someone who lived on the opposite coast…Regardless of the fact that he wasn't even what I was looking for—a stable guy with a stable career—my brain couldn't shut off. I thought about him constantly. The sensation of his tongue flicking against my clit, his fingers pushing inside me as he sucked my nipples, his cock pumping in and out between my legs…*this was why I wasn't supposed to have sex with Tony in the first place.*

All logic shut off when I connected in orgasm and I couldn't help but feel a sense of attachment to him. Apparently, it's not my fault;

it's science. When women have sex, our bodies release a chemical, oxytocin, (known as the love hormone), which increases our feeling of attachment to whoever (or is it whomever?) we have sex with. The more sex we have with that person, the deeper the feelings of attachment become. So, no matter how much women try to have casual sex, our biology is working against us.

Now that I was no longer Hysterical I could get back to my quest for *the one*. Let's face it, I was lonely, and the adventures of the dating world were more satisfying in my imagination than in reality. I wasn't wired like Kelly. I could never hook up with a random, in order to let go I needed to feel close and safe. I was able to with Tony because we had a history, years of friendship, and a connection.

After Tony returned to LA I decided to give the vibrator a try… that seemed like a more reliable replacement…so I decided to get familiar with Mr. Rabbit and keep my inner animal on a leash for the time being. I had way more important things to think about than boys and sex; I had to focus on getting my play together for the Cherry Lane One-Act Festival. It was only two months away and I had work to do!

MAY | GOOD GIRL

"Are you planning an overdose?" I scolded Kelly.

The last thing she wanted to deal with while tripping on molly was me getting all parental on her. But this was uncomfortable, and I didn't know how to be cool.

~ ~ ~ ~ ~

The first time I ever tried drugs was with my best friend, Sean, the beginning of our first year in university. Sure, we tried weed in high school, but it wasn't Sean's thing; he didn't like anything that slowed him down. The first time we did coke was in his parents' basement during the Toronto Film Festival before we headed to Yorkville where the celebrities sometimes hung out...in case we ran into Jack Nicholson or something. I know he's kinda old, but we were film buffs, and Jack's a legend.

The last time I spoke to Sean was four years ago, a year after I moved to New York and a few weeks before he had a cardiac arrest and went into a coma. He was diagnosed with a rare neurological disorder just before I left Canada and had been in the hospital ever since. I wheeled him around the hospital in his wheelchair, going fast and poppin' wheelies down the hall to the lounge. The stark fluorescent lights weren't very forgiving and the sterile smell made me a little nauseous. He had lost a third of his body mass and he'd been a skinny guy to begin with. It was hard for me to see him like that, but

I swallowed my sadness, determined to keep his spirits up and show him a good time. I was sure the last thing he needed was another teary-eyed face looking at him as if he was about to die.

"I almost died you know!" he blurted out as we got to the lounge.

My heart stopped. I never realized how severe his condition was. He kept it from me. I sat down on a chair across from his wheelchair and looked into his eyes. They were glazed over from all the medication he was on.

"You know I've been on drugs every day since I've been in here. Pills, IV, shots, you name it."

I took a breath. "So, I guess you're who I come to now for a fix," I joked.

As he looked at me, his smile faded quickly. "I don't know if I could ever do drugs again, when I get out. We used to run around all over the city looking to score, the strip club, the Gayborhood…That first year I came out, we must have been high half the time."

"That was a couple of years ago, and it wasn't all the time, and it never got in the way of our grades or our goals, " I interrupted.

"I'm not judging. I love all the memories and experiences we had. I just don't know if I ever could again, because for the past year all I've been dreaming of is the day I can exist without any drugs, the day I can just be myself."

There was a long silence. I looked down at the floor because looking in his eyes would have made me completely crumble and that's not what I was there for.

I quickly changed the subject. "Did I tell you my roommate, Kelly, is now a dominatrix?"

~ ~ ~ ~ ~

Over the past several weeks Kelly's man, Drew, was always at our place. In contrast to his crawl space in the loft/recording studio in Bushwick, our apartment was like a five-star hotel. Drew was awkward and creative. He tidied up after himself, cooked for us, and always entertained us with music and fascinating stories. I enjoyed having him around. He also kept Kelly distracted the right amount, so I could get my play up to speed for the festival that was quickly approaching.

Kelly was not only a genius, she was talented at everything from photography to art to fashion design, so she and Drew were always collaborating on one of her projects, and I would frequently end up their model/victim, depending on their vision. They set up elaborate decorative settings in the living room and photographed me draped in material dripping with paint. They used my frame to design garments and sew them onto me. I loved the attention and how they fussed over my makeup and hair. It made me feel special, and we got some really cool art pieces out of it, photographs, sculptures and clothing.

One sunny spring Saturday in May, Drew and Kelly took a hit of molly for breakfast at noon. They whipped up a gourmet brunch of Grand Marnier French toast and Gruyere and spinach omelettes that neither of them touched. Then they decided to design a new dress for Kelly to wear that night and pleaded with me to be their mannequin. In someone else's world that might seem random, but things like this were the normal reality living with Kelly. I insisted on actually eating their feast and instructed them to find their materials and get started without me. It always took them over an hour to gather their tools, pinking shears, paint, pin cushions, choose a color scheme and sort through the silks. One time, Kelly left me half-naked and sticky on a tarp on the roof for forty-five minutes when she was looking for her extra camera battery. They were the creatives, but I had become a pretty sharp production manager working with them. At this point, I wouldn't let her start anything until she had all her ducks (or duct tape) in a row, because I was the one who would get fucked if she missed a duck.

They were finally ready for me close to three o'clock. Gorillaz' "Dare" was playing, Kelly's favorite song to listen to while rolling. I was in Kelly's tornado-struck room with material and empty boxes of take-out scattered across the floor, when Drew got a phone call. It was the singer from his band, Edward, inviting us to a party for a record label in a suite at the Royalton Hotel. The dressmaking project was abruptly abandoned. Kelly and I tore through our closets searching for the perfect outfits for the night. Drew sat back and watched, commenting every so often on what worked and didn't work. I opted for a jean mini-skirt, vintage tank and leather belt, with some killer boots. Kelly sported her leather mini with red suspenders and black electrical tape Xs over her nipples, a sheer black blouse, and a leopard print jacket over the get up. We were so punk rock. It didn't matter to us what Drew wore, but we could tell he wanted some attention, so we dressed him in a funky get up, with an ostrich feather boa, crazy glasses and a pimped-out cowboy hat. We were ready to head out on our adventure.

"Wait, we can't forget the molly." Kelly pranced around, already high. They each took another hit of the stuff and gave me some. I took half in the bathroom and put the rest in my pocket. I wasn't nearly as adventurous with drugs as I had been before Sean got sick, but once in a while I did get the itch to go a little crazy. Even when I did have the balls to experiment, I always took half at a time; you can always take a little more, but once you do too much there is no going back.

We crossed over Ninth Avenue just as the drugs surged through our veins and headed east across 49th Street to avoid the crowds in Times Square…Way too bridge and tunnel for the kind of night we were hoping for, also a huge cluster fuck of cops and homeland security—all the people you don't want to see when tripping balls. It was a beautiful night outside, but we were too high to notice. We navigated our way toward Sixth Avenue; the lights of the city twinkled, the sidewalks sparkled and traffic was at a standstill. The exhaust from the idling cabs and their obnoxious honking filled the air. We continued down the yellow brick road to see the wizard. Well, with all the yellow cabs jammed up Sixth Avenue, that's what it looked like.

We arrived at the Royalton hotel around nine o'clock. We casually made our way to the elevator without drawing attention to ourselves, even though the three of us were flying high and flamboyantly dressed. The hotel was dark and mysterious, like out of a David Lynch movie, and I had this feeling like something outrageous was on the precipice of happening. The door to the suite was ajar so we let ourselves in. There were about a dozen people there, all stylish and attractive artsy New York types. We fit in just fine. The suite was large, with two bedrooms, two bathrooms, both with Jacuzzi tubs and a huge living/dining room area and full kitchen. There were dark blue drapes separating the rooms lit with dim blue lights. The entire hotel had this vibe as if it were designed for heroin addicts. I don't even know what I meant by that, but that's how it felt at the time.

Drew introduced me to Edward, the singer from his band. Edward was a hot Asian guy with long black hair, blue highlights and the right side of his head shaved. He was skinny, yet muscular, and had an arrogant swagger about him. I found out later from Drew that Edward was also a trust fund baby from Connecticut pretending to be broke, well, living like a broke musician, in a loft with five other *fake broke* musicians decorated with furniture off the street and milk crate shelving. Edward introduced us to the host, Thomas, a record label exec footing the bill for the night. He was tall and lanky with black eyes and a black curly mop, wearing a hipster style bright blue suit and skinny tie. He was gracious and directed us to the bar, offering us refreshments. There was a fully stocked bar in the kitchen with jumbo-sized bottles of booze and mixers. Thomas pointed out the dining room table, set up with seven silver platters holding not snacks, but an assortment of pharmaceutical drugs: small blue pills, large white ones, yellow gel capsules, and tiny pink ones. Each one had a place card in front of the tray with a description labeling the type of drug, suggested dosage, and what not to mix it with. There was everything from Adderall to Xanax to Valium to OxyContin… everything from anti-anxiety pills to pure synthetic heroin.

I was already flying high and still had more molly in my pocket so I was cool and completely anxious. Didn't anyone do old-fashioned coke anymore?

Kelly and Drew each grabbed a couple of Adderall, Xanax and Valium. I quickly pulled Kelly aside, concerned.

"Are you planning an overdose? Or just a murder?" I cautioned her.

"Don't freak out, Mom. They're for later. For like the rest of the month, or week, or whatever." Kelly asserted, annoyed with my reality check and proud of her findings.

"This shit is scary, it's not for partying," I whispered in a stern voice.

Kelly tried to shrug me off. "You gotta chill out, I know what I'm doing."

"No, you don't! No one does with this shit." I wasn't going to keep arguing with her, but for the record, I was not cool with the drug buffet.

Kelly suggested I grab a few treats myself, since it was open season on the silver trays. No way! I didn't care that they were free and open for the taking, I was not into it. Pharmaceutical drugs are way stronger than street drugs and way more addictive. Call me old school, but I really don't get the whole designer drug trend.

And, sadly, aside from the outrageous silver tray table of drugs, the party was pretty lame. Everyone was in his or her own high, isolated world. The molly had me itching to dance, so I found my own spot near the window with a view of Times Square and danced by myself—until the drugs started to trail off. I had no interest in taking the rest of what was in my pocket. Once the high wore off I would head home.

After a few moments, I looked over at the couch and noticed Edward staring at me with his head cocked to the side and a disapproving look on his face. He approached me.

"Wanna ditch this place and go somewhere we can really dance?"

My eyes lit up. I nodded and followed. He whispered something to Drew and we made our exit. We walked across town to catch the subway back to Brooklyn, where his roommate was spinning at some neighborhood bar.

Sure, Edward was sexy, but hooking up was the last thing on my mind when I arrived at the party. I got my fix in my first dirty fling with Tony; that was enough for now. That immediate need to have sex was satisfied. I was ready for a meaningful relationship. I was sure I could hold off for while, before my vagina started calling the shots again...

Edward lured me out, into his trap, away from my friends, into his bars in Brooklyn, his drinks, his incessant clamor of highly intelligible irrelevant jargon. The paradox of what I couldn't stand and what made me wet. After a few moments of banter, we hit the dance floor. I unconsciously flailed my body, grinding and thrusting to the 80s retro night delights in an almost empty joint in Williamsburg.

Edward offered me some powdered sugar, so I followed him to the bathroom. Taste after taste in the stall, the powder coating our egos, he kissed my cheek and then the next cheek, followed by my lips. He pulled me out onto the now-crowded dance floor and spun me around. The floor was mine and a stage it became... all the players fell in line, tapping heels, waving hips, thrusting, grinding and a wave of disco harmony made the moment. He wanted to dip me, what he really meant to say was take a dip in me, with me, pin me, sin me. He spun me around and threw my body back, my leg wrapped around his waist tightly. His hands briefly wandered along my bare thigh, powder blue satin panties exposed by the denim mini riding high.

I pulled away, he pulled me back. I could feel his tongue pressing against the pucker of my lips, forcing its way in my mouth. He stole several more kisses by the time we reached the basement of his loft. He seduced me, grabbed me in all the right hidden places; he made my chest rise and fall with anticipation as my nipples awoke.

In the basement living room, he put on a vinyl record—his band, of course—and then gave me a copy of it. He cut some more lines on an issue of *Rolling Stone* magazine resting on the coffee table. When they disappeared, he flipped through the pages to show me the write-up for the album he just gave me. His music was good, but if he thought an album and a write-up in *Rolling Stone* were all it took to get me excited he really had the wrong girl. Not to mention I'd already seen the article and heard his music, since Drew was in the band and practically lived at my place. It was cute the way he was trying to impress me, though. Unfortunately, he had no idea what I went through with Russell or that I was done with musicians. But I was open to fooling around a bit, since the drugs made me frisky. #WWKD?

Lying on his bed, clothed, we explored each other's surfaces, kissing deeply, licking each other's lips. I nibbled and sucked on the length of his tongue as he slipped it in my willing mouth. As the temperature rose, we slipped out of our sweaty clothing. My powder blue satin panties and matching bra were to remain on...only a few minutes longer. His teeth scraped against my collarbone, sending shivers through my body. His hands caressed up my torso, along the grooves of my rib cage, teasing me into longing. He gently cupped his hand around my breast as his lips quickly met mine, he caught my bottom lip between his teeth just enough to sting, then quickly released and licked my top lip. Every cell in my body was alert. Blood rushed in places I never felt before. His touch was both confident and cautious, never quite grabbing me where or as hard as I expected, causing my body to twitch in expectation and frustration.

A tiny sigh escaped from my pursed lips. He rolled on top of me and separated my legs. He was completely naked, toned, and strong, and his excitement stood up proudly. He pressed himself against me, holding my nipples between his fingers pinching them. He moved the tip of himself against the powder blue satin covering my treasure. He kissed my lips again, sucked on the top, then the bottom lip, as I teased his tongue with mine. He rolled off of me, bringing us both onto our sides facing one another. His hands wandered down my belly and another tiny moan escaped. He traced his fingers over my blue satin panties feeling the damp material on his fingertips. I closed my eyes and tried to relax as he rolled the satin out from under me and pulled it down past my knees.

I was wet all the way down my thighs; he followed my juice back to me, up my legs as my body arched, pressing my erect nipples straight into the air. Just before his hand met my waiting tenderness, I stopped his hand with mine and whispered, "I am not going to have sex with you tonight."

Arrogantly, he defended his cool. "I'm not desperate; I don't need to have sex with you."

I felt we had an understanding and he pushed his hand past mine and slid his fingers along the outside of my slippery lower lips. He quickly found my panic button and began to play me as he did one of his songs. He asked to taste me, to lick me, I refused him, afraid to lose control. I took his excitement in my hands and in my mouth; he grew even more. I sucked him hard and deep and soft and slow, over and over, until he grabbed me and brought my lips to his mouth. That made me even more excited. He brought his hand back to the stream of juice that now ran down between my cheeks and he followed the smooth liquid front to back. I collapsed with pleasure onto my back, arching into his fingers.

"Ooooohhhh…" I let out my first uncontrolled moan.

"Good girl!" he praised my reaction.

I gasped.

"Good girl!" Edward encouraged me as I bit my lip and dripped my excitement onto his fingers. He brought his slippery fingers to his mouth and sucked on them slowly tasting me. "Good girl," he whispered softly as he encouraged me again.

I wrapped my arms around his neck and sucked on his tongue, teasing it, nibbling ever so lightly on the tip. He continued to vigorously play my body like a mad protégé, moving from one erogenous zone to the next, eager not to miss a note. A grin washed on my face in sheer ecstasy, with each passing stroke wild pleasure filled me, consumed me, and his simple encouragement, *good girl*, sent me flying. I lay there, quivering, as he begged to be let in.

"I was wrong before, I need to taste you, to be inside of you, I am literally begging you for it. Please." He pleaded with me. My, how the tables had turned! Mr. I'm-too-cool-with-my-review-in-*Rolling-Stone*. Lucky for him his skills were beyond what I'd ever felt before, and I had no choice but to surrender to him. I'd already exercised an enormous amount of control, especially considering the ecstasy and cocaine. But what truly made me weak were the two words he kept repeating as I was overwhelmed by pleasure. "Good girl."

Good girl. That night, those two words changed my entire sexual life. That was the first time I had been encouraged to enjoy pleasure. I'm not sure about you, but I often had some sort of guilt floating around my stomach that came immediately following pleasure. I don't know why or where it came from, but I always had a sense of uneasiness. Maybe shame, maybe feeling dirty, I couldn't quite put my finger on it. Not that time. That time, I felt validated, encouraged to enjoy myself. I wasn't made to feel guilty about wanting pleasure. In the past, I'd always associated the words *bad girl* with sex. Russell would always refer to me as *bad* when I liked things that he did to me. Or when he wanted to try new things it would always be referred to as *bad things* or me being a *bad girl*. Edward put a whole new spin on sex for me. It was *good* that I felt pleasure, it was *good* that I was aroused, it was *good* that I aroused him. With those two words my hang-ups about sex began to fall away. It was liberating.

I never slept with Edward again. I randomly saw him at a couple of parties over the years. His band never went much further beyond that article in *Rolling Stone*. He partied too hard and burnt out quickly from the New York indie rock scene. It also turned out that he had a girlfriend, with whom he was conveniently on a break that night. Sure, I felt bad for the girl and wouldn't have done it out of sisterly solidarity if I was aware she existed. But I didn't care about Edward. I was surprised I didn't, but it was pretty simple: I didn't want him for more than a night. I got what I was looking for in the moment and was happy to move on. I had more important things to focus on: my career and my play. Was this what it felt like being a man? Or a *woman* instead of a girl?

JUN | LOST

"Are you gonna report him to the police?" I said as the room became icy.

Silence.

One night, Kelly arrived home around two a.m. to find me munching on a snack in the kitchen. Drew was at a gig and stayed at his own place for a change. I looked up from my cookie and could sense something was wrong before she crossed the threshold.

"Have you been crying?"

"I'm fine." She tried to avoid me.

"Is it Drew?" I pressed.

Silence.

I stared at her, my eyes demanding words. Kelly never cried.

"Max." A tear fell from her eye.

Yuck. Her ex-boyfriend who I couldn't stand who moved in with Kelly as I moved out to live with Russell years back. He and Kelly had only lived together a few months when he got a job in Indiana and moved away. He was an accountant and probably one of Kelly's only boyfriends that had a real job.

"Did he die?"

"I met him for a drink tonight," she explained. "He was fixated on seeing me while he was in town on business, regardless of how many times I turned down his invitations and explained I was in a relationship. He was relentless with phone calls, texts and emails. 'Come on, just one drink, I'd love to see you after all these years…'"

Max called himself a free spirit, but I would have called him more of a perv. He always barged in my room or the bathroom without knocking and then thought I was the one with a problem when I got upset. He got inappropriate with me more than once, but blamed it on being drunk or high. I never told Kelly. From my experience in those situations the girl always sides with her man. I know, it's so stupid, but most of the time, true. I didn't want to cause a rift between Kelly and me. And I didn't tell Russell because I didn't want him to go to prison for killing Max, so I removed myself from the situation entirely and moved in with Russell in Queens.

"I finally agreed to meet him for a drink so he would leave me alone. We met in his hotel lobby in Times Square, just a few blocks from home. If I wasn't with Drew there would have been no hesitation to meet Max for dinner, but I really like Drew, more than I generally let myself like a guy, and didn't want to hurt him by seeing an ex…So I made plans on a night Drew had a gig and wouldn't be around. No need to upset him with the past." She continued, "I headed to meet Max at eight p.m. I didn't fuss over getting ready so I wouldn't give him the wrong idea. He greeted me in the hotel lounge. We embraced. He looked exactly as I remembered, just a little more polished. We caught up over mixed nuts and martinis for about an hour. I was tipsy from the strong drink on an empty stomach. When I tried to excuse myself and call it a night, Max grabbed my arm aggressively and forced me to sit down, pleading with me to stay for another drink. For some reason I did. One more quickly turned into two and as another hour passed, so did my sobriety and faculties."

I didn't know where this was going. What could have happened?

"I remembered how much fun Max was to hang out with; he was more aggressive than Drew and had really matured since I last saw him. His hands wandered up my legs as he flirted and suggested I come back to his room. He even said he thinks about me every time he masturbates. Can you believe him? But I held my ground. It was after ten when I got up to leave. I can usually hold my liquor, but I was in bad form. As I stood up to say goodnight, the last thing I remember was falling face first on the floor. It all went black from there."

Wow. I didn't know what to say, so I let her continue.

"The next thing I knew I woke up in Max's bed with him on top and inside of me. I had no idea how I got there, what transpired between the lobby and the hotel room, or how much time had passed. I turned my head and saw the clock read 12:20 as Max kept penetrating me. I was missing over two hours from my memory. I lay underneath him as he pounded me quickly. When he finished, he kissed me and whispered in my ear, 'I miss you.' All I could think of as he pulled out was, *thank god he used a condom.*'"

I always hated Max; I always felt a darkness about him. I wanted to chime in, but she was so distraught, I knew it wouldn't help. I silently listened.

"I was totally disoriented, I went to the bathroom and showered. I wanted to punch Max in the face and kick him in the nuts so hard his penis fell off, but I had no recollection of how we got naked. I had my suspicions, but there was no proof that he forced me. I clearly recalled telling him I didn't want to go to his room several times. As I washed my body, I felt sick, not from the alcohol, from not knowing how I ended up in his room. I am a great fuck. What kind of creep even wants to have sex with a girl who is so gone she's lifeless?"

The answer came to her as she washed her vagina and noticed she was bleeding.

"A rapist. That's what he is," she concluded in a somber tone. "Other girls might have thought it was their fault, for drinking too much or leading the guy on, but as soon as I saw the blood it was clear that the sex was not consensual. Even when I'm drunk out of my mind, I still get wet when I'm horny…and if I was wet and horny there is a chance it might have been consensual. Blood means one thing; he forced himself on me when I was unconscious, or barely conscious."

I was terrified and shocked. I didn't know what to say or how to be supportive. I resolved not to say anything until she finished. I understood this wasn't easy to talk about.

"I got out of the shower, toweled off and got dressed. I was silent the entire time. I ignored Max, who was watching TV on the bed and went for the door. 'No kiss goodbye?' he said, trying to be cute. I smiled, walked over to the edge of the bed and sat down, leaning in. I pretended I was going to kiss him as I snuck a pair of handcuffs out of my bag and expertly had both his hands restrained to the headboard within seconds."

Shit! I couldn't help but wonder if he was still restrained to the bed. I sure hoped so.

"It's a confusing place for me. I'm promiscuous and sexually liberated. And he is someone I've already had sex with several times. For the past couple hours, I've just wandered the streets, lost, searching for answers, trying to put the pieces of what happened together in my head."

"Are you going to report him to the police?"

Silence.

"I'll come with you," I said as the room became icy.

Kelly glared at me with tears in her eyes. "No."

"You have to," I pushed.

"I can't. What happens when they ask me about where I work?" she snapped.

"That has nothing to do with it."

"Or why I met him at a hotel…"

She didn't have to continue. I understood. A dominatrix meeting her ex for drinks at a hotel and ending up drunk and in his room is not exactly the most convincing account of rape. I know a woman's profession and her clothing do not equal consent or an invitation for rape, but the reality is sadly different. When a police chief was asked to talk at my school, York University, about campus safety, following the escalation of rapes and attacks on female students, he told them, "If you don't want to get raped, don't dress like sluts." This statement was the catalyst for the entire SlutWalk movement, where women took to the streets in slutty attire to protest the ignorance of that statement. Subsequently the SlutWalk movement spread globally.

I had never seen Kelly so shaken. We both sat silently in the kitchen for what seemed like a lifetime. All these years living in New York as independent women we knew there was danger lurking in the dark corners of the city, but neither of us had ever faced them, or even felt them before. The most frightening part of the ordeal was that it happened with someone Kelly knew and trusted. Rape rarely happens at gunpoint in a dark alley with a stranger; most commonly rape occurs when a woman is alone with a man she knows and possibly trusts.

That night Kelly decided it was time to make a change. She wasn't sure how or what it would be yet, but she knew it was time. She didn't report Max. She didn't tell anyone about the rape except me. However, that night she resolved that she would never be a victim again and hasn't had a drink since.

JUL | MODEL EMPLOYEE

"Dinner? Opera? Like a date, Henry?"
My insides started shaking.

My one-act play was a success in the theater festival. I met many other talented writers and directors and was even offered the lead in a new play opening the following season from a connection I made there. Rehearsals wouldn't start until the fall, but it was nice to have something to look forward to. It also encouraged me to stick with the writing. Even though I started writing for personal reasons, to process my emotions, people seemed to be interested in my stuff and it was opening doors.

That summer I started writing more frequently in my spare time. I'd been caught up in a whirlwind of emotions over boy drama with Russell, Tony, and Edward, Asher and Trevor, and even David and Doug. There was too much swirling around in my head; writing was all I could do to stay sane. I wrote a couple more short plays, but, for some reason, most of it was coming out in poetry—naughty poetry. The first dirty poem was after I was drunk in the van with Asher.

My boss, Henry, kept me busy at work all summer. Henry's last relationship with the model ended in the Hamptons Memorial Day Weekend; she left him for a photographer she worked with on a

Victoria's Secret shoot a while back. When the model ran into the newly single photographer at a pool party, all bets were off for Henry.

Henry was handsome and oozed charisma. He was funny, educated, and well-read, but the girls he dated seemed more interested in the gifts and trips than his substance…and he always fell for the eye candy. He loved models, and they loved his socialite lifestyle. He could put anyone's Instagram to shame, only he chose not to have one, or flaunt his life in general, minus the occasional article about a business deal or high-profile breakup, like the one he was currently experiencing.

Over the years, Henry took me to all sorts of events: groundbreaking ceremonies, fashion shows, charity dinners and museum galas. I was used to accompanying him to events or out with clients. I was happy to go; I genuinely had a great time with him. He took me to some incredible restaurants and parties with such eccentrically fascinating people.

By mid-July I had developed a little crush on Henry. I knew it was so wrong; office romances are never a good idea. But we were spending a lot of time together after work and he was always sweet to me, treating me and paying for my taxi or Uber home. I guess that would have been one advantage of dating an older man, someone who's had time to figure out how to treat a lady and, let's face it, his finances didn't hurt, either. A struggling musician can either pay for your cab home or buy ramen noodles and a couple frozen pizzas to last a whole week. How could you hold it against them? This made Henry seem all the more spectacular. I wasn't looking for anything with him, but for now I was happy to enjoy the fantasy. It felt safe.

Henry and I were at a loft on Broome Street that was due for some renovations. He owned the building and wanted to remodel before he rented the unit again. As he wandered around the space I took notes on what he wanted to update. Henry kept glancing at me in a new sort of way, all morning. The sexual tension between us had been mounting since we left a meeting on the Upper East Side. I was in a short, yellow summer dress; we were battling 100-degree temperatures. The thin cotton fabric clung to my sticky skin.

"You don't have plans this Thursday, do you?" he asked as he grinned.

Just me and the rabbit, who had become a trusty tool to keep my hysteria at bay, I thought to myself. It was Monday. I shook my head, then remembered. "That's your birthday, right?"

He nodded and flashed a sexy smile. "Have dinner with me? I have opera tickets and reservations at the new Japanese fusion place on the Upper West Side."

"Like a date?"

My insides started shaking. Henry inviting me out was pretty run of the mill, but it was always to accompany him to some obligatory engagement or to grab dinner after working late. It was always under the context of business. The proposition made me nervous. I really liked my job, and I really needed it. It was perfect for my schedule of sporadic auditions and bi-weekly rehearsals at the theater company, and he paid me really well.

"You wanna spend your birthday with me?" I deflected sarcastically to dodge the discomfort of the situation.

"You already know all my drama, I know yours. We both need a fun night out. Let's have some fun, you and me, no pressure, just a good time. What do you say?"

I couldn't tell if he was asking me on a date or not. It didn't matter. No matter how attracted I was to Henry, I would not get involved with my boss. Especially because he was rebounding and my whole livelihood could be screwed up. I've already played out this fantasy in my head, repeatedly, I always ended up fucked—and not in the orgasmic way.

"Isn't Michael Kors having a show around the corner? Can't you just order one of his models for the night?"

"Ouch! Yeah, I probably could. I could order one in every color. But I was hoping to spend the evening with you. We already get along so well."

"Didn't anyone ever tell you about getting involved with your employees? It's not a good idea." I made my way over to the kitchen to avoid eye contact.

He could never be truly interested in me, I told myself. *He dates models and I am no model.* Why was he messing with me? Henry clued in that he was making me uncomfortable. He followed me into the kitchen and locked eyes with me, but before he could say anything, I said softly, "I really like my job. I wouldn't want to do anything to jeopardize it."

Henry's eyes stayed locked with mine as he nodded his head in agreement. "I need you more than you realize. You are the best assistant I've ever had. I enjoy your company, you're smart, and you can keep up with anyone I put you in a room with…I can't say that about most of the girls I have dated lately. Let me take you out to a show and a nice dinner. Not a date, nothing romantic, just a way for me to say thank you, for never letting me down."

I smiled in agreement.

"Terrific!" he exclaimed.

I could handle Henry taking me out as a thank you for my work, but going on a romantic birthday dinner with my boss was too weird, even if I did have a crush on him.

I took Thursday afternoon off to get ready for my non-date with Henry. He gave me a gift certificate to the spa to get a massage and my hair and makeup done. He really did know how to treat a lady; it was *his* birthday, not mine. I hopped between the eucalyptus steam room and the infrared sauna for a half hour before my deep tissue massage was scheduled. The entire experience was heavenly. I felt like a new woman after the massage, then the beautification began. They gave me a deep conditioning scalp treatment and then they proceeded to blow-dry my frizzy locks to a smooth, voluminous mane. After that I was escorted over to the makeup bar and the artist worked her magic all over my face. The two stylists turned me around for the big reveal and shazaam, I looked spectacular. These two angels had just proved my theory that, after two hours of professional hair styling and makeup application, anyone could look like a supermodel.

I thanked everyone at the salon profusely and tried to tip them, but they all refused and said Henry took care of everything. Wow. This guy was more and more impressive. I felt so special walking out of the spa I splurged and took a taxi home. I didn't want to mess myself up before Henry saw me.

I was tearing through my closet, looking for an outfit appropriate for the evening, when Kelly and Drew surfaced out of her room from a nap.

"Hi honey. Drew made some delicious pastries if you want some," Kelly cheered as she poked her head in my room. "Holy fuck! You are gorgeous!"

Her voice went up in surprise.

"Thanks," I said quietly.

"Drew, you have to come see this!" she shouted across the apartment.

"Damn, girl!" Drew blurted out, almost as if he didn't mean to.

They both insisted that they needed to do a full-blown photo shoot with me looking the way I did. I tried to explain that I had to get ready, that I had somewhere to be, but they ignored me and started snapping their cameras as I got ready. I tried on a few different outfits, ultimately wearing something Drew and Kelly chose. They forced me up on the roof and snapped shots with the city skyline in the background. The pics actually turned out to be a good idea; we got some amazing shots up there and one of them even ended up in a gallery show a few months later. I guess that kinda makes me a *model* in some weird way.

Henry and his driver picked me up at seven to head to the opera at Lincoln Center. The driver stepped out and opened the door. Henry was in a tux. He hopped out to greet me and took my hand and kissed it. My tummy was full of butterflies.

"Wow. You are a beauty."

I scrunched my face nervously.

"Thank you. It's amazing what a little bit of makeup can do," I deflected.

Henry could read my discomfort and tried to stop staring at me. I thanked him for the spa package and told him how excited and grateful I was for the entire experience. He insisted it was the least he could do and that he was overdue in thanking me for my work. He ushered me into the back seat of the black sedan and we sat next to each other in silence for fifteen blocks up Tenth Avenue. The only time I had been to the opera was when Russell took me to the free one in Central Park on our first date. I had always dreamed of seeing the real deal. His driver let us out right in front of the steps at Lincoln Center. I had passed by the building so many times, imagining for years what it would be like to experience the magic that took place inside, on that stage. I was giddy with anticipation.

Henry led me through a sea of well-dressed patrons; we made our way through the doors and were escorted to our seats on the balcony. The music commenced and the curtain rose for *La Traviata*. It was all like a dream. I was literally on the edge of my seat the entire performance. I noticed Henry watching me as intently as I watched the stage. It was like he saw me for the first time that night. I could tell something changed in the way he looked at me. In truth, it was disappointing. Couldn't he see how special I was without all that makeup?

The opera was the magical experience I hoped for; the costumes were elaborate and the music was moving. I thanked Henry again as we made our way back to his waiting car. We continued further uptown to a new Japanese restaurant Henry was sizing up; he always wanted to know the best spots. Henry ordered us a bottle of sake, seared scallops, and miso eggplant to start. I was starving and had to pace myself with the sake or I knew I would get into trouble. Henry downed the rest of the bottle before the appetizers arrived; I was still sipping on my first little cup. The appetizers were cooked to perfection. We both ate quickly and I was trying to divert his attention from the alcohol he couldn't seem to get enough of. I had spent a lot of time with this man and many dinners for that matter; something was wrong for him to be guzzling sake the way he was.

"Are you alright?" I inquired, concerned.

He planted his lips on mine before I could even react and whispered in my ear, "The model and that sleazy photographer are sitting at that table at two o'clock. I know this is completely inappropriate and I respect what you said. Please, just play along?"

I looked into his sad silver blue eyes and went from being royally pissed off at him for crossing a line I made clear I did not want to cross to being totally sympathetic in about a millisecond.

I kissed Henry again and snuggled up close to him. I knew the last thing he needed that night was rejection being rubbed in his face. I couldn't imagine being a wealthy, handsome, successful, affluent man in my fifties and still dealing with the insecurities of dating. I was twenty-five and didn't know how much more I could deal with myself. The thought of another thirty years of dating was terrifying, I wanted to be long settled down on the way to being a grandmother by the time I reached fifty-five. The rich playboys are a different breed; they like the action of the chase as each shiny object passes by, and they enjoy the option of juggling many girls, but when they're between girls it must get pretty lonely.

As soon as he pointed out his ex and the man she left him for, I was all over that scenario. I was cuddling with him, feeding him, letting him feed me…I'm an actor; I did stuff like that for roles all the time. Maybe I took it a little too far because while we were on dessert, I noticed that our audience had left, and Henry was three sheets to the wind.

We were finishing up when this hunky man approached our table to say hello.

"Hello Henry, nice to see you." By his greeting, I could tell he worked with Henry in some capacity.

"Join us for a drink!" Henry slurred as he motioned for this guy to join us. "Bryce is our IT guy. You know each other, right?" Henry added.

So, this was Bryce. I sized him up quickly. Early thirties, 5'10", light brown hair, blue-green eyes, pronounced jaw line, straight white smile. I'd had a working relationship with Bryce for over three years.

Bryce was in charge of all of Henry's IT needs: websites, social media, you name it. He also did graphic design and computer networking for us. He was a computer whiz and owned his own boutique firm. We talked on the phone at least once a month, whether I needed help on a network, updating a website or just a new graphic in a pinch.

Bryce was always polite and friendly on the phone, and, let's not forget, flirty. He was very generous with his time. He even gave me phone tutorials to improve my own website and navigate through Photoshop when I was designing flyers for the theater company. He had come to be a friend and a huge support even though we had never met face to face and it never occurred to me to Google him.

Bryce looked at me, searching for something familiar. "I don't think so."

"We've never met face to face, but you saved my life on a few occasions." I smiled.

"You're the assistant?" Bryce smirked as he studied me, trying to sort out the situation between Henry and me. "Nice to finally meet you, Dana."

"The beauty of cyberland. It connects everyone in the world in a way that no one ever has to make any real contact," I flirted.

"What are you drinking?" Henry interrupted.

"Thanks, Henry, but I'm going to call it a night," Bryce politely declined.

"Here alone?" Henry inquired.

"Yeah, I was putting out some fires for a client in the area and had a late dinner at the bar. I've been wanting to try this place for a while…"

"Shit, I'm fucking wasted," Henry interrupted. All the alcohol sunk in and Henry finally realized he was gone. "I am so sorry kids, I need to get home."

He slipped me his credit card to take care of the bill; I went over to the server and settled things. As I got back to our table, Henry stood up and handed Bryce a hundred-dollar bill.

"Make sure she gets home safe, please," he demanded as he hugged me and kissed me on the cheek. "I had a great night. Thank you for joining me. I'll see you in the morning." He staggered out the door where his driver was waiting for him.

Awkward…and now this attractive man was standing before me with the task of escorting me home.

"You don't have to take me home; I can call an Uber. I'm a big girl," I joked.

"You're actually a lot smaller than I pictured," Bryce teased. "It's nice to finally meet you." He took my hand and kissed it. I blushed.

"You, too."

"I'm sure you can take care of yourself, but I promised Henry I would get you home safe, so you're pretty much stuck with me until you get there."

"Okay, I'm in Hell's Kitchen, I'm sure there's a cab around. You ready?" I asked.

Bryce shook his head. "Not yet. It's a beautiful summer night. Want to go for a walk? I've been curious to meet you for a while."

My eyes sparkled at him! I didn't think anything would be able to top a day of pampering and a night at the opera until Bryce happened along…

Bryce and I left the restaurant and walked toward the Hudson River. We were both a little tipsy. Our hands found each other and our fingers intertwined as we strolled along like we had been a couple for years. We already kinda knew each other and I felt familiar. I'd been on the other end of the line through a few of his meltdowns and he for a few of mine. I knew about his family in Portland and his younger sister away at school. He knew all about my Canadian childhood and my work in the theater. He was also technically paid by Henry to escort me home safely; it wouldn't serve him or his firm to fuck with me.

Hand in hand, we wandered down the West Side Highway along the water past the Boat Basin down to Riverside Park, giggling and enjoying the sultry summer night. By the time we got to the mid 50's Bryce pulled me in to face him and I smiled slowly as our mouths inched closer together. I closed my eyes as our lips met and we kissed for a long few moments, almost hesitantly. Our lips separated, and he took my hand and led me towards Hell's Kitchen.

"Let's grab some pie, yes?" he suggested sweetly.

I nodded and followed him. I didn't even need to think about #WWKD; this one was a no brainer.

We wandered across town to Ninth Avenue and found a twenty-four-hour diner. It must have been after two a.m. We got a booth and Bryce ordered warm blueberry pie with ice cream. We danced in the empty restaurant to doo-wop coming from the old jukebox, twirling around and laughing until the pie came. We snuggled and sipped milkshakes slowly as we enjoyed each other's company. I was amazed at how sweet this guy was. In my experience guys as successful and good looking as Bryce were total dicks. They have a sense of entitlement, are infuriatingly narcissistic, and have very little regard or respect for others. Bryce seemed genuine, considerate and attentive. I didn't know what to make of it. I knew he valued his position, but this was above and beyond just getting me home. Could this guy actually be interested in me? No way. He's too successful, too smart and did I mention just too attractive to be interested in me. Then I remembered: I had undergone an extreme makeover earlier that day. He wasn't looking at the regular me; he couldn't see me past the eight pounds of makeup and the snazzy hairdo I was wearing. Now it made sense.

We detoured through Times Square before going back to my place. I would have wandered up to the Bronx if it meant I could stay next to Bryce longer.

"This is me," I sighed as Bryce's lips almost barely brushed against mine and he presented a single red rose that seemed to come out of nowhere.

"Do you wanna come in?" The words just escaped my mouth without me realizing it.

Bryce nodded. We made our way up six flights of stairs, stopping intermittently to steal kisses. I tried to sneak into the apartment quietly so we wouldn't wake up Kelly, but she was already up.

"So how was the date?" She charged into the kitchen with her robe open, her nudity completely exposed. "Did you sleep with your boss? I want to hear everything," she demanded, then noticed Bryce standing next to the refrigerator and pulled her robe closed, which was a rare event.

"This isn't Henry! Where did this guy come from?" Kelly was confused.

I introduced Bryce and explained what happened, that he was paid to escort me home. I invited Bryce to stay for a glass of wine and opened a bottle I had stashed for something special. Kelly got out two wine glasses and poured herself a soda. We settled at the kitchen table to relax. Drew was already passed out in Kelly's room; she'd worn him out for the night.

It was 3:30 a.m. when Kelly excused herself. I told Bryce he was welcome to crash for the night. It was late, we were tipsy again, and I liked the way he felt and smelled. I showed him my room and went to go wash up. When I got back, he was sitting on the bed in his boxers and T-shirt. I was wearing a pink silk slip.

"I hope you don't mind; I didn't want to sleep in my clothes," he explained.

"I didn't expect you to," I giggled and sat on the bed next to him. He held my face and kissed me.

"Much better," he said, caressing my cheek with the back of his hand.

"What?" I had no idea what he was talking about.

"You look much better without all that makeup. I can finally see you."

We lay back on my bed and spooned over the covers. It was hot and stuffy in my room even with the air going. He kissed my neck and shoulders, his hands wandering up my legs and across my thighs. I could feel his breath in my ear and the warmth of his body against my skin. I needed to be held. It felt tender and comforting. We were entangled in each other's embrace until morning. He never tried to fool around with me. I couldn't help wondering…whether or not he was gay. He didn't try a single move and the only thing in his way was a thin piece of pink silk. I had to stop myself. I couldn't go blaming homosexuality on every guy who didn't try to sleep with me. Maybe there were actually some good ones out there.

Bryce was awake by a quarter to eight. I gave him a towel and directed him to the shower. He insisted on taking me to breakfast before we headed to work, so I put myself together, threw on a cute floral summer dress, and we walked to the bakery nearby on Ninth Avenue.

"Thank you for such a fun night," I gushed.

"Yeah, it was an easy hundred dollars," he joked.

"And for being a perfect gentleman."

"I'm no pro, I only do freebees," he winked. "I think you're great," he continued.

"Me too, I mean you," I cut him off. "But since we both work for Henry, it might be kinda…you know."

"I was hoping you wouldn't say that…but I had a feeling…"

"I'm sorry," I pouted at him playfully.

"I'm kinda bummed," he shrugged.

"Me too."

We agreed to stay friends and parted ways.

In the past few months I had dated many men—all different types, backgrounds, levels of education, from all over. I had dated creatives, intellectuals, and executives, and it was hard to come to any conclusions. Each individual was just that: an individual.

After the whole model makeover, I started thinking, even though I got a little closer to having the Beth wow-factor, I would never be *that*. But maybe that was okay; maybe I was my own brand of sexy. I was attracted to all different types of guys, so hotness didn't have to come in just one flavor. That was the day I realized, model or not, I was my own flavor of hot.

AUG | THE INTERNATIONAL LANGUAGE

"Kelly, can you *please* keep your voice down?"

I half-shouted, half-whispered at Kelly as she drew the attention of the entire room to my nude figure.

In August auditions were picking up after the summer lull. I put more time into doing my hair and makeup and bought a few new things that were more revealing than usual. I felt sexy when I wore them, instead of vulnerable, the way I used to feel when I dressed sexy in an attempt to attract a guy. Now, doing it for myself, I felt powerful from inside and was proud to show off a bit (and it was sweltering outside).

Tony resurfaced after a short hiatus and was keeping me distracted with a slew of dirty texts about how much he wanted to devour me. Ever since our fling we texted/sexted from time to time and he kept inviting me to Los Angeles to visit him. A getaway to La La Land seemed like a fun adventure. That's where Sean and I always dreamed we'd end up. Plus, a change of scenery would do me good. I wanted to escape the city for a while and some dirty fun with Tony wouldn't hurt, either.

I scoured the net on a daily basis looking for a cheap flight to LA. I finally found one for the second week in September. I just had to hold out another month and then Tony could take care of business. I had come to terms with the fact that finding a partner was going to take a bit more time. In the meantime I had Tony to keep me distracted. Until another distraction came my way…

Kelly and I were seated in a small Thai restaurant in Williamsburg. I had just finished an audition in the area and she was heading back to the city from Drew's place. We were munching on Pad Thai and shrimp rolls when she dropped a bomb.

"I'm going to go to law school. I took my LSAT last month. Don't worry, I'm staying in New York."

I was surprised, but ecstatic. "Are you kidding?" It was hard to believe after knowing her all this time.

"Just please don't say anything to Drew. I know he won't be happy about it and I need to tell him in my own time."

I nodded in agreement.

"Turns out only lawyers make lawyer money. I can't do this forever; after a few years the whole *dom* scene has gotten pretty boring. I need a new challenge," she smirked.

I was so proud she'd finally come to her senses. She was turning twenty-seven that year; it was time for her to broaden her horizons. Well, okay, her horizons were pretty broad, but I was happy she'd decided to go down the path of intellect, instead of whipping men with a fetish for deviance.

Then, all the sudden, out of the corner of my eye I noticed a smoldering hottie…in a red polo shirt and navy shorts with a European air about his style. He had wavy brown hair, deep brown eyes, and adorable dimples. He walked across the small room to a table with his friend, an attractive man with wild blond curly hair and a slender build. Kelly and I couldn't help but glance over, studying the situation, trying to guess who they were, what they did and where they came from. We were being silly, giggling and joking around, making up stories about who they could be and where from. But, as soon as my eyes met his, this guy stood up and approached my table. I was shocked that he was coming over to me. My heart raced, as he got closer.

"Can I join jou?" he asked with a thick, sexy Catalonian accent.

He was direct and decisive.

"Sure," I said, blushing as he pulled up a chair, leaving his friend alone across the room.

Guys have a different code than girls do. Guys are always allowed to abandon each other in any situation for the possibility of pussy. Most women aren't as understanding about dick.

"I am Santiago. I am here from Barcelona for a month working," he said in broken English as he sat down next to Kelly, his eyes never leaving mine.

"Hola," I smiled nervously.

"Very nice to meet jou bot," he flirted back.

"Your friend can join us too; you don't have to leave him by himself," Kelly added.

Santiago motioned for his friend, Claudio, an Italian photographer, to join us. We all ate lunch together and Kelly suggested some less touristy attractions she thought they should experience. We were impressed with both these guys; they were smart, educated and sophisticated. They talked about their respective homelands in contrast to America. When the check came, Santiago picked it up, walked over to the server and paid for everyone's meal. Very classy.

As Santiago swaggered back to the table, he reached out his hand. "Come with me, I will chow you my estudio and my work."

Hesitantly, I put my hand in his and asked, "What kind of work do you do?"

He confidently announced, "Painting, esculpting."

I couldn't help but blush. I looked back at Kelly and she shot me a *don't even ask me of course you're going with him look*. #WWKD. Kelly thanked Santiago for lunch and excused herself, she had an appointment at the Waldorf Hotel and didn't want to be late.

Half the time Kelly would get clients that preferred a fancy hotel room to the dungeon in Chelsea. The clients would only spend a few hours in the room with her, if that, and she would get to hang out until check-out time the next morning. She could charge whatever she wanted to the room; so she had a romantic night planned with Drew after the work was done. I liked Drew, but I couldn't understand how he was okay with it all...spending the night in a hotel room with his girlfriend that is being paid for by some other man who was just there with her, doing naughty things. That was a little too dysfunctional for me. I guess it was the power that turned Kelly on, and Drew was the submissive.

While Kelly headed across the bridge, I was left with the two sexy European artists. I went to the studio and saw some spectacular pieces Santiago had created. The loft was filled with his work. The floors were covered with paint cans, brushes, tarps and canvases; the walls were cluttered with pieces drying. There were paintings of classical women's figures on industrial wood and metal scraps like car hoods and old doors. I find talent very sexy and this guy was oozing talent.

Claudio disappeared upstairs as Santiago and I talked about his inspiration. He had penetrating eyes; I felt like he could see through me right to my soul. I was nervous being around him. He was stunning in a dark, mysterious way and he was so dreamy.

It was warm in the studio. He offered me a drink. I studied his chiseled chest and biceps through his tight red polo golf shirt as he handed me a glass of chilled rosé. We clinked glasses, staring deep into each other's eyes. His energy was as intense as his stare.

Santiago grabbed a handful of my hair and smelled it, and then pulled my head back. I gasped. His lips pressed hard against mine, then he gently bit my bottom lip. I dropped my wine; the glass crashed on the floor as the rosé splashed at our feet. Santiago looked into my hazel eyes and threw down his own glass of wine; it crashed to the floor. I was startled and a little frightened and so terribly, wickedly aroused. We kissed in the middle of the studio, surrounded by spilled wine and broken glass. His lips were smooth, and his touch filled with passion.

It was late in the afternoon and I had to be at the theater to help paint some backdrops. I politely excused myself after Santiago and I made plans to meet the next day, Saturday, for brunch and to go to the Met. We kissed passionately one last time in the studio and then he walked me to the subway. He kissed my hand. "I am looking very much forward to our brunch tomorrow," he beamed. I blushed and ran down the stairs to the train, completely elated.

I met Santiago the following morning at eleven. He picked a super trendy French bistro in the Meatpacking District where many socialites hung out. The crowd was a little annoying, but the food was so delish it was worth climbing past the botoxed faces with their designer handbags and vintage couture. When I arrived, the place was crowded, and he was already seated at a lovely table by the window. He was even better looking than the day before; was that even possible?

He stood up to greet me and kissed my hand, I went weak in the knees. He smelled delicious, like hot cocoa. We had a lovely brunch, but my stomach was so filled with butterflies that it was hard to eat. He turned down the complimentary mimosas that came with brunch, commenting on how he didn't understand how anyone could start drinking that early. He should have seen Kelly on a Sunday in the old days. I was happy that he didn't want to spend the day buzzed; it was an indication that he was more interested in getting to know me than getting in my pants.

After brunch, I took Santiago through the West Village to the legendary Magnolia Bakery, famous for its scrumptiously sinful cupcakes. We bought a box and continued walking across town through The Village, peeking in a few vintage shops along the way. We crossed through Washington Square Park, and stopped to watch the chess players, musicians, and performance artists. There was a vendor selling roasted nuts and candy apples. Santiago had never had a candy apple, so naturally we had to share one. We sat on a bench gnawing at the apple as its sticky juice ran down our lips and fingers. He licked the juice running down the corner of my lip as I licked my sticky palm. The apple dropped on the ground as we began licking the sweet taste of candy off of each other..

By three o'clock we reached the south end of Central Park at 59th Street. The museum was roughly twenty blocks north, so we cut through the park, taking the scenic route. It was a sunny day and the park was crowded at every turn. We wandered through the paths in the park, stealing kisses and holding hands. We climbed a few of the gigantic rocks to look out into the city and passed by the pond with the sailboats. We came across a gazebo where we sat for a while, kissing and looking into each other's eyes.

We arrived at the Metropolitan Museum of Art at around four o'clock. I gave Santiago a run-down of the different sections. We went to see the sculpture gallery first. He educated me about his craft and the different types of material he worked with, who inspired him, what he dreamed of creating. It was exciting listening to him talk about his work. It became apparent that he came from a long line of artists and had a true respect for his process. I had never heard a boy talk with the passion and conviction he did. I guess it wouldn't be fair to call him a boy; he was just one year younger than me, and he truly was a man. The more I learned about him, the more I wanted to know, and the closer I wanted to be to him. We explored the museum for hours then perused the gift shop, where we stood flipping through art books. He offered to buy me a scarf he noticed I had my eye on. I thanked him, but politely declined when I realized how pricey it was.

It was dusk when we left the museum, still light enough to walk back through the park. We came across a carriage and he suggested a ride. I melted into a puddle of goo. I'd always dreamed of an old-fashioned romance and going on a carriage ride through Central Park. I looked him in the eyes and sighed, "Yes!" enchanted by the offer. He negotiated a deal with the driver and we climbed in. We snuggled close to one another. Santiago opened the box of cupcakes we bought earlier and fed me one while the horse clippety-clopped through the winding paths of the park in the warm August night. We took turns taking bites of the sweet snack and, when it was finished, I licked the icing off his fingers and he leaned in and licked the icing that was left on my lips.

He leaned over to the bag with the box of cupcakes in it, and presented me, not with another cupcake, but with another small box.

"I wanted you to have dis," he said as he handed it to me.

I looked down at the box and took it from his hands carefully; it was the scarf I was admiring in the shop.

"Thank you," I said softly with my eyes fixated on the deep blue shades.

Santiago took an end of the scarf in each hand and looped it around my neck, pulling me in closer, brushing his lips against my neck, then went back to talking about art. I found it arousing just listening to him speak with such passion in his sexy accent. I loved that he wanted to share his thoughts and ideas with me. He was a perfect gentleman the entire carriage ride. It was refreshing; most of the New York guys I was used to meeting would have tried to get me to go down on them in the carriage.

We were famished after the ride; it was after nine and we hadn't eaten anything but cupcakes and candy apples since brunch. We headed downtown to a delicious place in Little Italy where I knew the chef. Over the years with Henry I'd collected a few connections of my own. We got off the train in SoHo and crossed over to Mulberry Street. Roxy and I worked together when she used to be a cook at Henry's restaurant; now she was the Head Chef at this great little place called Amarone.

The cramped space was crowded, so we sat at the bar and Roxy sent over a couple of glasses of wine while we waited. The atmosphere was alive and buzzing with an eclectic mix of bohemians, hipsters and suits. Santiago enjoyed taking it all in.

"The cultures in New York are so diverse, all living eside by eside," he observed.

The wine quickly went to my head because of my empty stomach. I began giggling. "Why do you laugh at me?" Santiago looked at me quizzically.

"I'm not laughing at you, I've had such a wonderful day, and the wine…"

Santiago cut me off with a kiss. As his lips were pressed against mine the hostess came to show us to our table.

I convinced Santiago to let Roxy surprise us with dinner, reassuring him that she was a friend and would make us a fantastic meal. We started with an amuse-bouche of lobster ravioli, followed by braised scallops in garlic butter and arugula salad for starters, homemade pappardelle with rapini and burrata for the main, then profiteroles with chestnut gelato for dessert. Roxy paired a lovely bottle of wine with the meal and everything was perfect, from the service to the way the food was cooked. I finally had my opportunity to impress

Santiago. From the look on his face, how he savored each bite, I think he enjoyed himself. After we finished eating, I insisted on treating him, as a thank you and to let him know I made a good living. He simply laughed and kissed my hand. "It's already taken care of, my dear." He stood up, took my hand and led me out the door.

It was clear that this guy was something special. The more time I spent with him, the more time I wanted to spend with him. I couldn't believe how much ground we covered in one day. I felt like we had been dating a month by the time dinner was over. This was only our first day spending time together, but it felt like each place we went was a new day and a new date…and as the day went on, I was falling harder and faster.

We briskly walked the streets towards the L train, anxious to be alone after dinner. I was a little tipsy and the world was swirling in a sea of vivid colors from the traffic lights and cars whizzing by. On the subway Santiago was cracking me up. He had a great sense of humor and was quick and witty with the comebacks. He mocked many of the people we saw and American culture in general, imitating things he'd seen in his best attempt at English.

When we arrived at the loft Claudio was already asleep. Santiago and I curled up on the couch and I felt happy. It was the best date I'd ever been on. As we started to doze off, we made our way into the bedroom.

"Would you like something more comfortable to wear?" he asked, offering me a T-shirt. He turned around to give me privacy as I changed. What a gentleman!

I took off my dress and let it fall to the ground, undid my bra and put on his T-shirt. I left my red lace panties on. He wore his boxers, and we snuggled up under the covers to a movie playing on his laptop, I can't even recall which one. We lay on our sides and I could feel his body running down the length of my neck, shoulders, back, ass, and legs. His feet rubbed against the soles of mine and his package pressed up against the red lace between my cheeks. He ran his fingers along my belly and my hips, tracing my silhouette with one hand. He kissed my neck slowly as I drifted to sleep tight in his arm and had the sweetest tasting dreams.

On the walk to breakfast Santiago told me about the art show he was in town to be a part of. He had already been in New York for two weeks creating pieces for the exhibit, and would be leaving town two weeks later, once the show opened. Of course. A guy this great doesn't just fall out of the universe from nowhere without a catch…I had extra respect for him explaining the situation before he slept with me, which is more than I can say for many American men.

I made the best of our romance while Santiago was in town. For the next couple of weeks, we traipsed around from one incredible experience to the next, gallivanting from little Italy to little India, Battery to Bryant Park and Park Avenue to Park Slope. I let things at work and at the theater company slide for a couple of weeks. I was playing hooky to spend time with my conquistador and I wanted to savor every moment I had with him before he left. When I wasn't with Santiago, I was tucked away writing seductive poetry, things I was embarrassed to even put on paper, but the urge to write was too compelling not to. Recounting stolen moments of pleasure, symphonies of panting breath, bodies anxious with wanting, craving the next moment. We had fooled around quite a bit, but we hadn't gone all the way.

One week into our romance I took the afternoon off work to see Santiago at his studio. He was wearing a pair of dirty trousers and a wife beater, both covered in paint. We kissed when he opened the door and he led me into his workspace. I was surrounded by his paintings of nude and mostly nude women.

"I wrote something, a poem. I would really like to share it with you, but I'm nervous." I hesitated.

He was intrigued. "Please, please read me your poem. You never told me you write poetry," he said, urging me to share.

"It's just something I do for myself. I've never really shared my poetry with anyone yet, except my best friend, Kelly, who we had lunch with," I explained.

"I am honored to hear your poem." He led me to the couch where he sat down eagerly waiting for me to recite what I had written.

CENTRAL PARK

Central park, almost dark
Bright city lights reflecting off the water
In the silence my skin feels hotter

Blood orange bursting sky
Glasses clink over sips of rye
The chill of night meets the twinkle in your eye

Rainbow leaves dancing in the summer trees
My heart flutters with the passing breeze

In the gazebo, passing by homeless people
I want to feel your churchless steeple

A city of chance
A taste of romance
Give me a glance of what's in your pants

Central park, after dark
It all begins with just a single, tiny spark

When I finished, he looked at me with his usual intensity. "Can I paint you, for my chow? I feel very much with inspiration every time you walk into my estudio and now you read me this poem, I must. You must let me paint you," he pleaded with me.

I was speechless. I took a long pause to consider it. This had nothing to do with sex; this was about creating art. He was the most serious artist I had ever met; he had such immense respect and passion for his work. How could I refuse him? If there was any tiny piece of me that truly believed that *I* was an artist, I would do it. Hell! If Botticelli isn't considered a pornographer, why would Santiago be?

~ ~ ~ ~ ~

When I first arrived in New York, I enrolled in a two-month acting intensive program at a prestigious conservatory on the Upper East Side. The first day was a disaster. After dance and voice class we finally had our first acting class. I was ready to work hard, to do whatever it took. I wanted to be great.

The male acting teacher slipped in the room and boisterously announced, "Everyone, stand up and take off your pants!" I looked around at my fellow classmates and the majority just laughed.

"Stand up and take off your pants," he repeated.

"You're not serious?" some voice asked sarcastically.

"Yes, I am," the teacher replied.

My heart sank. I couldn't stand in front of everyone with my pants down, in my underwear; I was wearing a see-through G-string. Maybe if it wasn't see-through and wasn't a G-string…wait a second, what a perv, why did he want us all to take off our pants? He hadn't even told us his name yet! One guy in the class did get up and drop his jeans. He was wearing plaid boxers. I bet you if he were wearing a sheer blue G-string he wouldn't have been so bold. This guy would go on to be the teacher's favorite for the rest of the program. The teacher continued the class with no explanation.

Later that afternoon I stormed into Kelly's apartment. I had been holding back tears since the mid 60s and was about to blow. I dashed into my room, hurled myself on the bed and began to wail.

Kelly rushed in after me. "Is an animal dying in here?"

"I hate acting school! My teacher is a dirty old perv!" I cried and the tears streamed down my face into the corners of my mouth.

"What the fuck happened?"

I recounted the story.

"You need to chill, girl. This is no big deal. It's only a matter of time before you all see each other naked anyway," she asserted matter-of-factly.

I looked at her, puzzled.

"…In the dressing room, backstage, doing a love scene. You are not a little girl in Canada anymore and Mommy and Daddy are not here. If you can't stand on stage in your underwear, you don't have a prayer of making it as an actress in this city, or anywhere else, for that matter. If you really want to be an artist, you are going to have to bear a lot more than that, honey. I think your teacher sounds brilliant."

Everything Kelly said made sense. Almost too much. One thing was for sure: I might have been in New York on my own, but in a lot of ways I was still very much a little girl, no matter how much it hurt to admit it.

It wasn't long after that I lost my virginity to Russell.

~ ~ ~ ~ ~

I took a deep breath and disrobed. Sure, Santiago had seen me naked, but in mid-action where we were both occupied with tasks—not like this, with his only task being to stare at my naked body and study it. Santiago set down a layer of colored pillows on the floor in front of a wall covered with velvet drapes and instructed me to lie across them. He approached me and kissed my nipples, giving each one a sharp bite to awaken them. He brushed his hands up against my thighs and grabbed my ass, studying my curves. I stroked the bulge in his pants and gave him a special kiss for inspiration. I lay there on the floor for several hours as we talked, and Santiago painted me. I recited some other poems he had inspired me to write. He kept asking to hear more and he shared some of his favorite Spanish ones that he knew by heart. I trusted him, and he opened himself up to me. He stopped every so often, turning away from the canvas to tease me and play with my body. We finally made love on the floor while he was painting me. And twice more after we were done: once in the shower and once in the bedroom on his desk and against the dresser, then we came simultaneously in the bed in the early hours of the morning.

I reached a new level of freedom that day and in a weird way I felt Sean with me; he was the only other person who ever told me I inspired him. Santiago and I had a deep connection. I felt like, together, anything in the world was possible…like magic. I couldn't keep up with my thoughts; remnants of pleasure sparks were surging through my veins for days after. I couldn't stop writing; I couldn't write fast enough. Ideas were flooding my mind. Something new had awoken in me, a curiosity. I had broken a barrier, a boundary I had set for myself, concerning my body. Nudity would have been an automatic 'no' just a few months or days earlier. But under the circumstances, the artist, the love affair, there was no way I could pass on this experience. I had to, not because I was following the rules—#W-WKD—but because I was following my heart.

The simple act of baring my skin for a painting made me realize I had been closed off to so many experiences because of a stigma that no longer existed. In the past, the scariest thing would have been for someone to find out about the painting and tell other people I knew.

But I didn't live in Smalltown, Canada anymore, and the only people who would really care, like my parents, would never see it anyway, so what was there to fear? And even if they did, it wasn't porn—it was art, and I was proud of it. I was a grown adult and I wasn't ashamed of my body anymore.

Those two weeks with Santiago were the best two weeks of my life. Every day was filled with adventure and possibility. We danced in the streets, laughed in bed, and got lost in each other's eyes. As our time together was coming to an end Santiago invited me to visit him in Barcelona. Although I knew from the start our time together was limited, I was really starting to get sad about his having to leave.

Santiago finished my portrait a couple of days before the gallery show. This man literally turned me into a piece of art. I was painted on a small door of an antique wooden cabinet that was two feet wide by two feet high. A painting of me sitting amidst the pillows, it was dark and shadowed. My skin looked flawless and radiant, my eyes glowed, hair flowed, my breasts looked supple and perfectly shaped. The curves of my body were enticing. I was breathless.

"Do you like?" he asked when he revealed the piece.

I threw my arms around him and, with tears in my eyes, replied, "I love!"

The night of the opening came and Kelly still had no idea about the painting. I was dying to see the look on her face when I surprised her. We headed out at seven and splurged on an Uber to Williamsburg, deciding we were dressed way too cute to schlep on the subway in the heat. In the car, I confessed I was sad about Santiago leaving. "I've really fallen for him."

"Just be happy you got what you did. Imagine, if we never went to that Thai place, the past two weeks would have never existed. You would have gone about your life and you wouldn't have even known what you were missing."

Kelly, my wise and crazy friend, was right again. Although there will be pain and tears, the experience was worth it. Damn worth it! The romance, the passion, the art created as a result, his paintings, and my poetry. In that Uber, approaching the gallery where my naked portrait was hanging on a wall, it occurred to me that pieces of magic are hard to come by, and that pieces are better than no magic at all. I had to stop putting so much pressure on myself and eventually all the small pieces would turn into the big picture.

We arrived at the gallery fashionably late, and the place was already crowded and buzzing with conversation. There were five artists being showcased in the exhibit, including Santiago and his photographer friend, Claudio. All the artists were European and had been invited to New York for a month by the curator to create new works for the show from their foreign perspectives. Kelly and I wandered around the gallery, admiring and discussing pieces that struck us. I sipped on complimentary champagne and Kelly sipped mineral water.

I waited for Santiago to notice me. He kept glancing over and smiling in my direction, unable to pull away from the cacophony conversation. Each time he became free another swarm of guests lined up to speak with him. I smiled back. I was proud of his work and he deserved all the attention he got for it. Claudio approached Kelly and me as we were talking about one of his photographs of Coney Island. Kelly was a talented photographer herself and they got caught up in a conversation about light. I excused myself and started snooping around for my portrait. There was a crowd gathered around it. I was nervous to go near it, afraid of being recognized. Finally, Santiago was able to break away from his fans and talk to me. He welcomed me with a kiss on either cheek.

"Congratulations!" I gushed.

He sold all five pieces he created within the first hour of the show. I was so excited for him until I realized my naked picture was going to be in some stranger's home.

"Someone bought me?" I asked him.

"You were pre-sold before the show. I'm taking that one back with me. That's why I painted it on such a small piece of wood," he explained.

I stroked the side of his face and kissed his cheek. "Thank you," I whispered in his ear. "You are the only one I want to have it."

"I was going to give it to you," he continued, "but decided if you want it you have to come to Barcelona to get it."

"Oh, my gawd!" Kelly's voice pierced through our quiet conversation. "Am I hallucinating, or are you naked in that painting?"

Kelly was in total shock and was much louder than I was comfortable with, especially because of what she was saying.

"SShhhh. Kelly, *please* keep your voice down!" I whispered forcefully.

Her mouth was agape, half in shock, half in admiration.

I eyeballed Kelly, mortified. "We don't need to announce it to the entire room!"

Kelly hugged me and held me tight. "I am so proud of you! And look how beautiful you are." She had truly become my number one fan. She always encouraged and pushed me to explore myself in new ways as an artist.

The show was winding down and Claudio invited us out for a late dinner so the four of us went back to that tiny Thai place where we all met. Santiago and I sat close while Kelly and Claudio sparked a little chemistry of their own.

Things with Drew were complicated; once Kelly stopped drinking and partying, the entire dynamic of their relationship changed. She became more focused on going back to school, but still hadn't told him her plans and the more Kelly tried to focus on the big picture, the less she saw Drew in it.

After a quick bite, we all headed back to their loft. There were a couple of bottles of bubbly waiting for us to celebrate their successful month in New York. Claudio sold four of his five pieces and gave the unsold one to Kelly. Both friends had triumphed on their trip abroad. Santiago turned on some music as Claudio popped open a bottle and filled three paper cups with champagne and handed Kelly a small bottle of Pellegrino. We danced and drank and laughed half the night away. I consulted with Kelly before retiring to Santiago's bedroom, making sure she could get herself home safely. She whispered to me, "I'm not going home" as she shot Claudio a look. I snuggled up to my lover for one last time as Kelly seduced Claudio in the other room.

Santiago and I made love slowly and tenderly several times until the sun rose and its rays peeked through the window shades. I confess I was daydreaming of moving to Barcelona with him and getting married and having his Spanish babies. We promised we would stay in touch, but we both knew it would never work out with us living so far away. But, even if this was just a brief affair, I was grateful for the experience, for the sheer pleasure of his company. With Santiago I started to feel a connection between my creativity and sexuality. Well, I guess I'd been feeling it for a while, but was finally able to put my finger on it. I started to own my sexual power with Santiago and to understand that sexual freedom and artistic expression were not exactly mutually exclusive. Those two weeks helped me realize more about what I wanted: someone refined and sophisticated, who challenged my mind and inspired my creative passion.

SEP | HOLLYWOOD NIGHTS

"Candice broke your penis? You really expect me to believe that?" I stood there looking at him cynically.

HE TOOK IT OUT!

My ticket to Los Angeles was booked for the second week in September, ten days after Santiago left. I was still caught up in our romance and wasn't sure if I was even interested in seeing Tony anymore. Santiago raised the bar for me. Were Tony's rugged good looks and dirty talk going to be enough? Sure, he turned on my body, but could he reach my soul?

I was filled with mixed emotions, but still excited to get away to Los Angeles, a place I had dreamed of going my entire life. Sean and I spent all of high school fantasizing about what it would be like out there…and I was finally going…without him, while he lay in a coma in a hospital in Canada.

I arrived at LAX on a sunny Wednesday afternoon. I collected my bags from the carousel and waited for the shuttle to grab my rental car. I flirted with the guy behind the desk and convinced him to upgrade my compact car reservation to a cute convertible for the same price. He agreed and handed me the keys to a bright blue Mustang with a black ragtop. LA was treating me well so far. I put my bags in the trunk and drove up the 405 Freeway towards Tony's place in Venice Beach.

I texted Tony to let him know I was on my way. When I pulled up to his house, he was outside waiting for me with a huge smile and a bouquet of roses. My hesitation dissipated…so maybe I was still kinda into him…and since we'd already slept together, it was like it didn't count, right? The old me would have felt guilty because it was still so close to Santiago, but the new me just wanted to have fun.

"You have no idea how long I've been waiting for those lips," he said in his thick, Brooklyn accent as I got out of the car.

He wrapped his strong arms around me and kissed me hard—so hard I could feel it in his pants. Tony looked the best I'd ever seen him. He had a tan that brought out the olive tone in his skin, his green eyes sparkled in the sunshine, and he had dropped a few pounds and toned up.

"You look great!" I exclaimed.

"Livin' by the beach, it's a whole different lifestyle. I go for a run on the sand every morning and the food out here is way healthier than grabbin' a slice on the go in the city. I can't even find a decent slice out here. I eat organic greens now, can you believe it?"

When I felt his chest, he got a little shy and backed away.

"You are lookin' good yourself. You can use a bit of a tan, but damn, you're hot." He diverted the attention away from himself, noticing I was a little more polished than he was used to.

He carried my things inside the house. He lived in a cute little bungalow off of Abbot Kinney with two other LA actor guys. The place had a rustic, bohemian feel to it. There was an overgrown garden that encompassed the grounds of the house, a couple of lemon and orange trees and a fire pit in the backyard with mismatched chairs and benches surrounding it. We continued to the back of the house to Tony's room. He set my things down and pulled me onto the bed. We kissed for a while and he still made me weak. After a few minutes of smooching we smoked some marijuana in the backyard and headed to the beach to watch the sunset.

What a scene; Venice Beach almost reminded me of a New York street fair on acid. Vendors were selling original artwork, jewelry, photographs, T-shirts, beachwear, essential oils, and incense. There were musicians playing, painters painting, and dance troupes entertaining the tourists and at least half a dozen weed shops.

The sea breeze was fresh and salty; the sun glistened off the water as it sunk low on the horizon. Crashing waves in the background drowned out the laughter and conversations coming from the boardwalk. Tony and I walked on the sand towards the water and sat down as the sun began to set. The sky was painted with vivid colors of orange and purple as the palm trees floated in the breeze behind us. Tony leaned in and kissed me aggressively, forcing me back into the sand as his hands wandered up my shirt. But my head wasn't there. I was tired from the flight and starving.

I pulled away.

"I'm hungry. Long flight," I explained apologetically.

"Of course, let's grab something."

We walked back to the boardwalk as the sun inched its way down, disappearing behind the ocean.

After some yummy vegan food, we went back to Tony's house. It was close to eight when we arrived, and both his roommates were home. Carlos, a comedian and SoCal native, was round and scruffy, like a teddy bear, and Ron, a martial arts champion from Russia, worked as a stunt guy. I excused myself to freshen up, but the jet lag was hitting me. I lay on Tony's bed and fell asleep for a half hour. Eventually he came in to get me.

"Hey, Sleepin' Beauty."

I woke up disoriented; it took me a minute to realize where I was.

"Can I jump in the shower?" I asked.

"Sure, babe." He grabbed a towel out of the closet and tossed it at me.

A quick shower helped wake me up. I changed into a BoHo influenced dress with strappy sandals, threw on some makeup and gloss. I met Tony and Ron back in the living room where they were watching TV. Carlos had already headed out to his gig at the Comedy Store on the Sunset Strip. There was a Chinese teapot resting on the coffee table with a few small ceramic matching cups. "Would you like some tea? It's mushroom," Ron offered as he lifted the teapot with a sly wink.

"Like shroom tea?" I had to clarify.

He nodded.

"Sure," I said, raising my tiny teacup with wide eyes.

We sipped the tea slowly, chatting about the Hollywood scene and what they suggested I do/see while in town. Once the tea was finished, we headed out to Santa Monica. The three of us couldn't stop giggling. The lights from the Ferris wheel on the Santa Monica Pier danced in the night sky and the moon hung low over the water. It was still very much summer in LA, and I was happy to be outside. As we made our way back to Tony's place there were scattered pockets of homeless people camped out for the night and the odd cyclist or skateboarder whizzed down the bike path. We came across a playground and each hopped on a swing; in the darkness it felt like I was swinging across the sky. The stars were gleaming, and the air smelled sweet of flowers and honey.

Later, Tony and I were in his bed trying to fool around but the shrooms were still in effect and we kept giggling at each other. I was too ticklish, and he kept making me laugh. Every time he touched me it felt like aliens were poking and prodding at my body. I felt rubbery and my senses were off. Tony tried for a long while to arouse me, but the trip we were on had clearly led us to different planets. I kept giggling as Tony huffed in frustration. Eventually I passed out.

The next morning Tony brought me a smoothie in bed when he came back from his run. I appreciated that he let me sleep in, especially since I wasn't much of a runner. I sipped on the smoothie in Tony's bed as he hopped in the shower. He came out of the bathroom wrapped in a towel.

"You sleep okay?" he grinned.

"Great," I replied.

"You like the smoothie?" he asked.

"Delish!" I sucked back a long sip.

He approached the bed and took the smoothie out of my hand and sat next to me.

"Can I have a taste?" he asked as he leaned in to kiss me.

As I raised my hand to put it around his neck, I knocked the smoothie out of his hands by accident, and because the lid wasn't secure, it spilled all over us and the bed.

"If you wanted to get kinky you should have just said somethin'," Tony joked, and he leaned over to lick the mess off of my stomach and thighs. He pulled my hips towards him and, as I fell back on the bed, I hit my head against the wall. We both started laughing. As he stood up to help, he slipped on the smoothie juice that dripped down on the floor and went flying, as I reached out my hand to catch him, I slapped him in the face. We were both half-laughing and half moaning in pain.

We cleaned up the mess from the floor, changed the sheets, and hopped in the shower together to remove the smoothie residue that was sticking to our skin. We lathered up, feeling each other's bodies as we kissed, but were cautious because we didn't want to slip and have a shower fiasco on our hands. After we toweled off, we returned to the bed and climbed into the fresh sheets.

Tony grabbed both my wrists and pinned them over my head as he straddled me and licked my lips. I could feel his chest pressing against my breasts. He ripped off the covers and kissed up the length of my body, starting at my toes and making his way to my neck. His hands caressing, his lips kissing and tongue licking. I was surprised; I wasn't that into it. Sure, he knew how to touch me, but my head wasn't in it. There was definitely something lacking in our chemistry. Tony could tell something was off and started fumbling. I didn't know what to do, or how to handle the situation, or how to stop him without hurting his feelings, so I imagined Santiago and tried to enjoy it. Our session was a very sad and sloppy scene where we just couldn't seem to find a rhythm. We were trying to go back to a moment that didn't exist anymore. I was no longer in a state of hysteria filled with pent up animalistic desire. Months before he'd been the second guy I'd ever slept with, and since then, I had slept with two more and evolved past our chemistry. I changed. The same things didn't work anymore. The sex wasn't bad, it just wasn't fireworks like it was the first time or like with Santiago.

I tried again with Tony that night. Things got better, but in no way could they measure up to the marathon we had in New York a few months earlier. He felt more like my buddy than a romance and I wasn't hot for him the same way.

I stayed with Tony for three nights. He took me to Malibu where we went on a hike in Topanga Canyon, then walked along the 3rd Street Promenade in Santa Monica. We mostly stayed on the West Side by the water. On Saturday I thanked him and headed out to Hollywood to explore the city on my own for a few days. We had one last sweaty go at it Saturday morning (what the hell, #WWKD!), and it wasn't half bad. I also had no idea when I'd have a chance to have sex again, so jumped on the opportunity.

Trevor and I met for brunch at a crowded place on Melrose with a backyard patio. We hugged for a long few seconds; he felt good, like I remembered. We caught up over eggs Florentine and huevos rancheros. He was gearing up to shoot a new studio film in a couple of weeks. As he was telling me about it, I was a little jealous.

"I would kill to be in a real Hollywood movie," I whispered quietly.

"You will," he replied, not sure what to say. "How's the writing coming?"

"Good," I responded.

Trevor treated me to lunch then I followed him to his house in Los Feliz, a total hipster part of town. He lived in a small house with another actor who was on a series shooting on location in New Mexico, so he pretty much had the place to himself. The house was on a hill and had beautiful views of the city and the Hollywood sign. We sat on the back patio and smoked a joint, reminiscing about the horror shoot. He was so easy to talk to. We connected really well.

Later in the afternoon we took a yoga class in Griffith Park. It was my first time doing a yoga class outside in nature and it made a lot more sense than how we all cram into a jammed studio in New York. After yoga, we walked up to the Observatory in the park and watched the sun set into the hills. The sky was orange and the air smelled sweet and pungent. LA certainly does sunsets well.

Back at Trevor's house we showered, separately. Trevor was in his room while I was getting out of the shower. He was wearing a robe, and I a towel. His body was perfectly chiseled. I got a little shy and nervous because it was new, or newish. I knew we had kissed before, but that seemed like a lifetime ago. I also had just had sex with another guy that morning…but I became curious at the notion of sleeping with two guys in one day. Something I never would have even contemplated before, but such an opportunity had never presented itself until now, so there was never a reason to consider it. I knew guys did things like that, or assumed they did. I knew Kelly had done it. Kelly did it a few weeks ago the night she hooked up with Claudio. They had sex that night/morning and then Drew was back in her bed that afternoon. I was curious to see if I could do it. As an experiment...or research. #WWKD.

Trevor came toward me and gripped his hand around my neck; drawing me into him, he kissed me sensually. I was apprehensive at first; his desire caught me by surprise. But his kiss was tender as his hand was firmly around my neck. His other hand released my towel, and it fell to the floor. He teased my body with his fingers and lifted me back onto the bed. I lay there naked for a long moment as he studied my body. He removed his robe and crawled over me on the bed, gliding his smooth skin against mine. Our lips met again as his hands wandered between my legs. My body arched back in pleasure, legs spread wide, eyes tightly shut as colors swirled around in my mind. His fingers thrust inside and my excitement dripped. I tried to push his hand away as he sucked on my tongue, but he continued as my body quaked in avalanches of pleasure. Once I came, he stood up and left the room.

"You should start getting ready if you don't want to be late. We have reservations," he smirked as he walked away, naked and hard.

Trevor took me to a delicious sushi restaurant, then to a party at his friend Anton's nightclub. The club was dark and crowded with celebrity and socialite types. I felt completely out of place, except for the fact that I had Trevor on my arm. He was attentive and didn't leave me alone all night, even though girls with very little clothing were flirting in his direction. Anton invited us into the office, where there was a huge pile of cocaine on his desk, and cut some lines.

Anton was hot in your typical LA hipster way. Cool clothes, cool hair, 6'2", and totally ripped. He owned a few businesses, including a clothing company and a trendy burger joint; this club was his latest venture. Trevor and I hung in Anton's office for a while doing lines, and the guys also did shots of Patrón. I decided to stick to one substance for the night. I'd never been a huge fan of mixing.

By one a.m. Anton invited us to an after-party at his friend's place in the Hills. We Ubered to a house off of Kirkwood, which was set back and built into the hills. Everyone there was blasted out of their minds. Lines of coke were being cut on the coffee table, breakfast nook, and dining room table. In high school Sean and I dreamed of coming to these Hollywood parties in the hills where everyone was doing coke, but actually being there didn't feel cool at all. It felt stupid, because it was all about the drugs. It didn't matter to any of these people where they were, who they were with, or what they were doing, as long as they were blasted. For me, drugs could enhance an experience, but for these people drugs *were* the experience.

A couple of girls started rubbing their bodies against mine as I danced; I could tell they were totally on molly. I heard some other people talking about Xanax and Adderall. This party was over my head. I was having a great time with Trevor, but I wasn't comfortable in this scene. Sure, I'd done my share of partying, and I'd been around all sorts of drugs, but this scene was the most extreme. I tried making conversation with some of the guests, but they were clearly on a different wavelength.

To my relief, Anton invited us to his place. It was close to three o'clock when we arrived at his house near the top of the hill with amazing views of both Hollywood and the Valley. The house was decorated with vintage retro décor and pop art on the walls. Anton turned on the stereo and sank into the couch, where he cut more lines on the coffee table. Trevor told some hilarious stories of crazy times they'd had together and I started to drift off on the couch.

At 4:30 a.m. Trevor woke me up in a mad panic.

"Wake up! I need your help!" Trevor shook me.

I jumped, startled. "What is it?"

Trevor was frantic. "Anton thinks he's OD-ing. I need you to clean up the coke!"

I jumped up in a daze, not sure what to do.

I panicked. "What happened?"

"I have to go get his neighbor, a doctor. The coke can't be there when he comes inside…but don't throw it out…"

Dude is OD-ing and they're worried about saving the coke? In addition to the eight ball he shared with friends, two hits of molly, some OxyContin, and Xanax to come down…Anton was sure it was the two Klonopin he took to go to sleep that put him over the edge. I wiped off the leftover coke from the table and stashed the rest in Anton's bedroom. I found some cleaning fluid under the sink in the kitchen and disinfected the surfaces. Anton was in the shower fully clothed and drenched in the fetal position vomiting intermittently. I got in the shower with him, also clothed, rubbed his back and encouraged him to keep puking.

That's where we were when the doctor arrived. I quickly slipped out of the bathroom to give them room, but stayed close enough to hear everything. The doctor looked at his eyes, listened to his heart, took his blood pressure and assured Anton that he was not going to die, and prescribed that he drink lots of water and once the drugs dissipated from his system he'd be fine.

"You should take this as a warning to slow things down, Anton," the doctor cautioned. "You're going too fast man, way too fast." The doctor exited the bathroom, obviously pissed off at being woken up in the wee hours of a Sunday morning.

I was traumatized by the whole experience. My first Hollywood party and I ended up in a scene out of a Quentin Tarantino film. We helped Anton get out of his wet clothes, put him in bed, and gave him lots of water. Trevor and I eventually passed out on the couch, fully clothed and a little damp, in last night's makeup.

We slept until noon and woke up to the smell of frying bacon. Anton woke up feeling like a new man with a new lease on life. He wasn't foggy or hung-over and was making breakfast: veggie bacon, eggs, oatmeal and smoothies. We ate breakfast and had a laugh about what happened, even though none of us really thought it was funny. We didn't know how else to deal with it. After breakfast Anton's girlfriend came over and we slowly made our exit once it was clear she would be sticking around a while.

We followed the winding road down the hill in an Uber.

"Welcome to Hollywood, babe," Trevor said as he looked over at me.

"So, is that the usual Saturday night in Hollywood?" I joked.

"Yeah, for some people. Not me though. I don't usually get into that shit. Last night was a one-off. That isn't my scene. Sorry I brought you along for that. Some host I am." He looked at me apologetically and held my hand.

"Are you kidding me? Now that no one is dead or anything, it's a fucking great LA story!"

Our smiles quickly faded because it wasn't funny. I was beat when we got back to Trevor's place.

"I'm gonna hop in the shower, I feel gross..."

I went in the bathroom, turned on the shower, took off my clothes and got in. Trevor snuck in behind me. His chest pressed up against my back as the water trickled down our bodies and he began massaging my shoulders. Trevor washed my body, caressing my back, my ass, my calves and thighs. I washed his back and chest and we kissed in the steam-filled shower. When we finished, he toweled me off and we snuggled on his bed. We didn't fool around; just lay there holding each other. I guess we both had a lot on our minds. After a while I got up and got dressed.

"Where are you going?" He sat up and watched me.

"I don't know. I need some fresh air. You wanna come?" I asked.

"I feel a little sick, I'm just gonna lay here for a while."

Things were distant between us. I know it wasn't anyone's fault, but we both needed some time to process what had happened. Separately. We didn't know each other well enough to do it together.

"It was great to see you," I said as I gathered my things.

"You, too. See you soon, I hope." He didn't question my leaving; the vibe was really weird and I needed to go.

I sat in my rental car and searched for a hotel room on my phone. I booked a room in West Hollywood for the night. I didn't want to deal with Tony or with anyone for that matter. I was looking forward to a peaceful night alone in a hotel room with nobody else's drama.

The next day I was driving across Beverly Boulevard towards Robertson when my phone rang. I answered it on my Bluetooth, without looking at the number.

"Hello?"

"Hey pretty baby." It was Russell, of all people.

"What do you want?" I demanded in a short, pissed off tone.

What the hell did he want? I hadn't spoken to him since he left me used and naked in that hotel room as he went home to his girlfriend, Candice. He had left a few messages during the summer, but I never responded.

"You still in LA?" he asked.

"How did you know I was here?"

"I ran into Kelly last night at a show, she told me."

Oh, great. *Note to self: kick Kelly's ass when I get back to New York.*

"What do you want?" I groaned into the phone.

"I'm in LA. Just for tonight. Come see me at my hotel, Chateau Marmont. You'll love it. Ten o'clock."

What was he doing in town? I couldn't see him. He was still living with Candice. Fuck! I wanted to see him. I still missed him, no matter how dysfunctional it was. But I didn't have enough time to process all my thoughts in that split second; I had to decide on the phone. After all that had happened, I still wanted him to want me, to love me...

"Fine," I said and hung up.

I arrived at the Chateau Marmont just after eleven, wearing jeans, a silk tank top, suede boots, and a leather jacket. Casual, but sexy. I pulled up and the valet opened my door. I gave him the keys and told him to charge it to room 712. This legendary Hollywood hotel and hangout to the stars is tucked away on a hill overlooking the Sunset Strip. The décor in the hotel felt old and rich. There were a few tables of people lingering in the restaurant and the lounge was crowded for a Monday night. As I got in the elevator the doors closed and a rush of panic came over me. What was I doing? Did I really need to subject myself to more of Russell's manipulation?

I walked down the hallway. I stopped, glanced in the mirror, reapplied some lip-gloss, flipped my hair a few times and continued to his room. I took a deep breath and knocked on the door. Russell opened it, wearing a pair of designer jeans and a plaid button-down shirt with all the buttons open so his chest and torso were exposed.

"Wow, you look great. Is it me or do you just keep getting better and better looking?" Russell tried to hug me as I walked past him and wandered around the room checking it out.

"I keep getting better." I said as I stared at him coldly.

A bottle of wine and some fruit rested on the desk by the window. I walked over to see the view. Russell stood next to me and opened the wine. There was an awkward tension between us. He clearly didn't anticipate me having any hostility towards him. He poured the wine.

I grabbed the glass from him hastily and took a long gulp, then helped myself to a strawberry.

"I miss you," he said, looking right into my eyes. "I can't stop thinking about you." He leaned in to kiss me.

I pulled back. "Really?" I questioned, not buying it.

He tried to kiss me again. Again, I pulled away. I hadn't even been there five minutes. What did he expect? I was there on *my* terms. Things were gonna be different.

"Slow down," I said forcefully. "So, what's going on? Why are you in LA?" I pried.

"Busy working. It's not the same as being in the band, but I'm making good money and still working with musicians, so it doesn't suck."

"You've really turned things around. It's nice to see you doing well," I said, forcing a smile.

"Wanna hear this new band I'm working with, Wake? They're pretty amazing…" He leapt over to his laptop on the nightstand and played me a few of their songs.

He was right, they were amazing. Way better than his band ever was.

"I've been working with them since the spring, coming out to LA a couple times a month. We had a showcase for some of the execs at the record label tonight at the Viper Room on the strip and they killed!"

"Nice!" *Thanks for the invite*, I thought to myself.

I was into this new band. My ass took over and forced me to dance around the room. Russell grabbed me and we grinded against one another; the music was so good I didn't want to stop him. We fell into old familiar ways and started kissing. Russell pulled my leather jacket off and threw it across the room. But once the music stopped,

I pushed him off of me, and he fell back onto the bed. I had to keep it together and stay in control.

"Aggressive. I like it." Russell was salivating lying across the bed. "Where are you going?" he whined.

"Thirsty," I said aloofly as I crossed back to the bottle and poured myself another glass of wine.

Russell shot up off the bed and approached me almost in desperation. "My penis, he needs you. He's broken," Russell blurted out.

"I'm sure."

"I'm serious, he is. You want to see him?" he urged.

"No, I don't. But thanks for the offer," I said, callously.

"I had an accident, with Candice. I'm serious." He was.

"Candice broke your penis. You really expect me to believe that?"

He took IT OUT and showed it to me. As much as I wanted him to be full of shit, he wasn't. It really looked damaged and had a scar running along it. Even at full mast, his once beautiful penis that proudly stood erect was now frightened and shriveled and scarred. What did Candice do to it?

Over Christmas Candice was riding him reverse cowgirl, his penis slipped out of her and she slammed down on it, folding it in half. Within seconds the fluid that filled his erection was all over them and he was rushed to the hospital. There are three tubes in the penis: one for urine and semen, and two that fill with blood in order to hold an erection. He had severed two of the three tubes and was rushed into emergency surgery. She literally broke his penis! He spent the holidays recovering and slowly, months later, he was finally starting to regain the use of his sidekick.

I felt horrible. All my plans for payback went out the window as I was filled with sympathy and compassion. After all, it used to be *my penis*.

Maybe his broken penis meant that I had a chance to get back in the picture? It was a year and a half since our breakup. I knew I should be over him, but the history was hard to shake, and all of the emotions came flooding back. He now had a good job and was settled and able to give me everything he couldn't before. I felt compelled to kiss his penis better, so I did. Gently, slowly, attempting to nurse it back to its former glory. My nurse routine led to a round of playing doctor. I was weak and let my guard down. I believed his broken penis meant we had a chance at a future, because it obviously wasn't happy with its current situation.

"You have no idea how much I need you. I think of you every time I touch myself. Dana, I need to be with you," Russell panted as he pulled me up off my knees.

I kissed him seductively, I ran my hands down his face and chest, over his ass and spanked him hard.

"This is a very sexy hotel room," I teased.

"I thought you'd like it," he said, as his eyes pleaded for me.

"I do."

I kissed him again and caressed his excitement gently. "So, Mr. Big Shot, what's the deal with Candice now?"

He began shrinking at the sound of her name. "Babe, baby," he stumbled over his words, "Look, don't get the wrong idea about tonight. You know I love you, but the timing isn't right for us."

"What exactly does that mean? That you want to live with your girlfriend in SoHo and keep fucking me? Because that doesn't work for me," I snapped at him.

"I'm sorry, I don't know how to tell you this. Candice and I are going to be married next month," he said sheepishly. He proposed to her hastily after the accident, afraid his penis would never be the same. Once on the road to recovery he regretted it, but couldn't backtrack without putting his job in jeopardy. Candice's father was both his boss and his landlord.

"Married?!" I gasped.

Everything started spinning; the world got blurry and I couldn't quite hear anything. I could barely breathe or think or move, but somehow I managed to gather my bag, jacket, tank top, bra, and boots and hurl myself out the door, almost clothed, with one boot on. Russell sat there, shocked I'd actually walked out on him.

How could I have been so stupid to waste four years of my life with that asshole loser? I put the rest of my clothes on in the hallway before making my way to the elevator, holding back tears with every inch of self-control I had. My breath was shaking, and my chest jumped with each short breath, as tears fought their way out of my body. My throat was strained and my nose filled with snot. I locked myself in the stall in the ladies' room in the hotel lobby, vomiting and sobbing for an hour. I was with him for four years and the word marriage never came up once!

Finally, I was all cried out, my face was red and puffy and my nose was raw. I looked at myself in the mirror and took out some concealer. I quickly touched up my makeup, just enough to be seen in public, and then planted myself on a couch in the lounge to figure out my next move. It was almost two a.m. I was a disheveled mess in the lobby bar of an exclusive Hollywood hotel. I had stupidly planned to spend the night with Russell. What was I thinking? Usually I'm a pretty sensible person. I dug through my purse searching for something, I wasn't sure what...I pulled out my pen and my blue leather notebook and began to write.

Ten minutes had gone by when four drunk, punk, rowdy guys stumbled through the lounge and tried to get some drinks. The concierge politely informed them that it was past last call. Three of them went up to their room and one, a quintessential surfer type, made his way through the lounge right past me, to the piano. I was engrossed, writing, tucked away on the couch. I didn't notice him and he didn't see me slouched over my notebook. I let out a sigh of frustration, a little louder than I intended, just as he passed me. "Uuuugggh!"

Surfer dude jumped back startled. I couldn't help but laugh.

"Holy shit, dude, way to freak a guy out! Were you just sitting there waiting to give me a heart attack?" he asked in a laid-back surfer drawl.

"Sorry," I said, laughing. This guy was adorable. Bleached Mohawk, deep, ocean-blue eyes, skinny but ripped, around six feet tall. He was wearing skinny jeans and a tank top where the sides were open so I could see his muscular arms and eight pack. He also had some sexy tattoos on his arms and shoulders.

"First you scare me, now you laugh at me? Real nice," he joked.

I was relieved to be laughing.

The dude continued over to the piano and sat down. "You mind if I play a little?"

"Please, I could use a distraction right now."

He fingered the keys, then started to riff.

"Wow, you're good. What are you playing?"

"Thanks. Nothing, just fucking around. What are you doing down here all alone? Waiting for your boyfriend or something?" he asked a little flirtatiously.

"Just writing, needed to get out of my room for a bit..." My head sunk into my hands.

"So, you're a writer or something? What are you writing?" he asked curiously.

"Or something. A poem," I responded quietly.

"Can I hear it? I would really love to. I am a huge fan of poetry, that's, like, what songs start off as?"

I was hesitant, but this guy was super adorable, and I needed the company, even if it was only for a few minutes.

"Sure," I said hesitantly.

WE ARE ALL ANIMALS

Hanging, on the edge of coming
Can you feel it, my body humming
With your fingertips my body strumming

Hanging on the edge of flesh
As our souls melt and mesh
Exquisite pain I can't express
With my eyes your soul I undress

Come and come and go
Come back and come again
Warm flesh in the snow
As your sex and treasure grow

Don't stop, even after we pop
Come again my love friend
'Till the end of this dream
As I scream
Our bodies flop like animals

We tear our bodies 'till we bleed
Trying to fill our savage need

"You wrote that? just now? That's brilliant. I love it," he said with enthusiasm as he leapt off the piano bench and sat next to me on the couch.

135

"Thanks," I blushed.

He stared at me intently. "Do you want to come up to my room...?" he asked.

"You're really sweet and all for saying you like my poem but I'm not looking to hook up..." I rambled on, too nervous to tell him off.

"No, I don't mean to fuck," he laughed. "You're hot and all, but I mean to come meet my band and maybe check out some of our stuff...our record label put us up here. We had a gig on the strip tonight."

I sat there silently, not sure how to respond.

"You're writing is fucking cool, I know Kevin would love to hear that shit...maybe it'll inspire us to write something sick."

"What's your name?" I asked.

"Josh. My band's called Wake."

Of course! Wake, the reason Russell was in LA...and this guy wanted to hang with *me* and said I inspired him?

"I'm Dana," I said, reaching out my hand.

He grabbed my hand and pulled me to my feet. "So, Dana, wanna come hang? You're a rad chick and a brilliant writer. I'd really love to chill with you, fully clothed. We've got some herb..."

I guess herb was the magic word. I went up to Josh's hotel room. They were staying in a suite with a living room in the center and a bedroom off to either side, and each room had two double beds in it. When we got in the room there was a layer of smoke in the air and Kevin was on the couch. The others were asleep. There were empty bottles of booze, soda cans, plastic cups, chip bags, and candy wrappers all over the place. A few guitars and a keyboard leaned against the wall in the corner and Spotify played on shuffle in the background.

Josh introduced me to Kevin, the front man, who perked up a bit with a guest in the room. They played me their album and I danced around the room. I gushed about how impressed I was with their sound, pretending I hadn't heard the album a couple hours ago in Russell's room. Kevin passed their three-foot bong over to me and I took a couple of mad rips.

"I would offer you a drink, but we're out," said Kevin.

"I'm cool," I said as I twirled around to their music.

When their album ended Josh insisted it was my turn to show them what I've got. I pulled out my blue notebook and flipped through.

"Do the one you just wrote," Josh instructed. I complied.

Kevin picked up his guitar and asked me to repeat a few of the verses. He played around, putting a melody to my writing while Josh watched smiling. After an hour of sharing our talents with each other, Kevin went to bed and Josh and I were left on the couch.

We spent some time getting to know one another. He talked about music and I about New York. We really hit it off. I almost forgot about the dagger that had pierced through my heart a few hours earlier. Josh and I fell asleep curled up on the couch together, not having even kissed. The next day I got my own hotel room on the strip a few minutes from the Chateau and Josh showed me around for the remainder of my trip. He took me to the Getty Center, a few clubs on the strip to hear some local bands, and a couple of great vegan restaurants. Hanging with him reminded me of when I first started dating Russell, my first taste of freedom, only this guy already had a record deal, so we were hanging in style.

Josh and I were alone in my hotel room my last night in town. We kissed impatiently trying to get each other's clothing off. He had model good looks and a body to match. We filled the bathtub and emptied the tiny hotel shampoo bottle to add bubbles. He turned off the lights, sparked a joint and we climbed in. We faced each other and my legs wrapped around his waist, his pelvis inches away from mine. He inhaled the joint and pressed his lips against mine, blowing the smoke into my mouth as he pulled me closer with his free hand. I exhaled the smoke and kissed him slowly. We passed the joint back and forth until it was finished. Josh flicked the roach into the toilet and sank back into the tub so only his head was visible. I moved back to the opposite end and stroked him under the water. His eyes closed as a grin took over his face. We fooled around in the tub until the water got cold. Josh hopped out first, wrapped a towel around his waist and then bundled me in one and carried me to the bed.

Josh tossed me on the bed and I leaned over to turn out the lights.

"Leave them on," he requested, "I want to see you."

I was still self-conscious about my body, but that had to be the sexiest thing a man had ever said to me, so I had to comply. Josh pulled the towel off of me and tossed it over the chair. He tossed his as well. He studied my body, my curves, my hips, my breasts. He opened my legs and pushed my knees back to study my sacred spot. His eyes widened as a smile spread across his face.

"Can you recite one of your poems while I go down on you?"

Correction, *that* was the sexiest thing a man had ever said to me. Juice was dripping between my legs; I was so aroused before he even touched me. Laying back on the bed I recited my poetry as Josh lowered his face to meet my wet lips.

Although I did pick up a box of condoms earlier that afternoon, I was fighting with myself in my mind trying to decide if sleeping with Josh was a good idea or not... especially considering I was leaving LA the following day and would probably never see him again.

Had I learned nothing from Santiago?

I still had to question, how much pleasure is one entitled to? I thought to myself. It's not like I wanted to turn into Kelly. I paused in that thought, in that judgment. Why not? Maybe I did. *Not to flaunt my promiscuity like she did, but to have fun and pleasure as freely... Yes, I did want that.* That was my final decision, so I went with it. No one was counting my number of sexual partners other than myself anyway. In the real world no one cares how much sex anyone is having unless they aren't getting enough of it.

Josh took my orgasms to the next level, as in multiple, like one orgasm wasn't even finished and I already could feel another one coming on. He was relentless, and I had no choice but to surrender to his hands, his mouth and his beautiful instrument. He was strong and flipped my body around with ease, as sweat poured off us until the sheets were drenched. I couldn't believe his stamina. He climaxed four times before morning and then another two before checkout. I did almost double that. The last two times we arrived simultaneously. He was a machine.

Our last morning was absolute bliss. I was awakened by soft, wet, open-mouth kisses covering my pussy. Josh's face was buried, feasting on the sweet icing between my legs. I was panting, trying to catch my breath, trying to control my body from contracting and trembling in sheer delight. His fingers explored me and his hungry mouth wouldn't quit. I tried to sit up and pull his head back, but he grabbed my neck gently and said, "Lie back," as his eyes hypnotized me. I collapsed back onto the bed. He continued to work my body, sweat dripping off of me as I died against his tongue. My body was damp and quivering as he crawled up to kiss me and whispered, "Good morning," in my ear.

After we finished our last round, Josh lay on the bed naked while I packed up my things. We ordered in breakfast to the room and said our goodbyes.

"I'm sure I'll be in New York soon for a gig. You will have to show me around that crazy city when I get there. I'm dying to check it out," he said.

"For sure, I'd love to show you around New York," I smiled, never actually expecting this relationship to go past the hotel room door upon exiting.

Josh and I said our goodbyes and he insisted we'd be hanging out in New York soon. I didn't expect to ever hear from him again, but we did the whole email/phone number exchange and followed each other's Instagrams.

"Yeah, I can't wait to hit up the clubs in New York," he said. "I was too young last time I was there, but now that I'm out of high school I have a few hookups!"

Out of high school? I froze. I knew Russell referred to them as kids but he was eight years older than me; I was a kid to him. Yikes! How old was this guy? Was this illegal? Could I go to jail for this? I knew he was younger than me but I thought he was, like, twenty-three. Holy shit. Deep breaths.

"How old are you?" I asked, trying to seem casual.

"Eighteen," he said casually.

Eighteen, I gulped. I'd never even dated a guy who was eighteen, not even when I was eighteen. Well, that explained his stamina. This kid had to be the most experienced eighteen-year-old alive. Plus, he was of legal age, so I couldn't get arrested.

OCT | HEAD IN THE CLOUDS

"Do I have to beg you for it?"

I groaned rolling around the rug naked in blissful frustration.

I got to LAX on a Thursday to find that they double booked my seat on the flight back to JFK. As much as I would have loved to hang out another day with a rising star, I was California sun fried and needed to get back to the reality of New York City. After waiting around an hour, they got me on another flight and bumped me to first class for the inconvenience. Not a bad way to end a rock star trip, in rock star style.

I sat next to a sophisticated-looking guy in his mid-thirties. He had brown hair speckled with a few stray grays, blue eyes, and an average build. He was dressed in a sport coat, T-shirt, distressed jeans, and a pair of Italian designer loafers. He wasn't friendly or interested in talking. But as the six-hour flight dragged on, he grew restless and began to engage in some banal conversation about the poor service on the flight. Peter was thirty-four, returning from a month travelling through the South Pacific. He worked at his father's real-estate development firm. I told him I was a writer. That was the first time I'd said that to anyone.

We shared a cab from JFK, and before he dropped me off at my place in Hell's Kitchen, we made plans for dinner on Saturday, two days away. He let me off at my stoop, grabbed my bags out of the trunk, set them on the sidewalk and kissed my cheek goodnight, then continued in the taxi up to his place on Central Park West.

I lugged my bags up the six flights of stairs and finally got into the apartment. It was close to midnight and I was beat. I couldn't wait to curl up in bed and process all the craziness that occurred in LA. I was happy to be back in my own space.

When I opened the door to the apartment, I could feel the tension from Kelly's room all the way in the kitchen. It felt like something was about to erupt.

"Kelly, are you here? Is everything okay?" I asked, approaching her bedroom door.

"Hey hon, can't wait to hear about your trip. I'll be right out," she shouted through the door.

"You are NOT going out there! We are NOT finished discussing this!" I heard Drew whisper forcefully.

"Don't grab me, there is nothing to discuss," Kelly shouted and stormed into the kitchen.

"What's going on in there?" I asked.

"I just got the LSAT results! Aced it! Guess who's back at NYU?" she squealed in excitement, jumping up and down.

"That's wonderful, Kelly, I am so proud of you!" I gave her a big hug. Wow, she really did it.

Dominatrix turned lawyer…how poetic.

"Being a dominatrix, I realized I enjoy the power that comes with fear and respect, I want to parlay that into the rest of my life. So, I decided I'm going to be a judge. Law school is just a stepping-stone… What have I got to lose, right?"

"Your soul!" Drew flamboyantly burst out of Kelly's room. "And me!" he continued seriously.

"Drew, you're overreacting." Kelly tried to calm him down, but there was no remedy for this. Drew was a recent NYU dropout himself. He was brilliant, like Kelly, but he was a lazy mooch. I didn't care how smart he was; Drew had become a waste of space. At first I thought he was weird and fun to hang out with, but as the months went by I grew to resent his lack of contribution to both our apartment and the world, his half-assed involvement in the band, the fact that he hadn't had a job the entire time I knew him, and that he was stingy with money, even when he had some.

Also, Drew was jealous of Kelly. The fight had nothing to do with her; it was all about his insecurities and losing his meal ticket. Kelly was more or less his sugar mama, but with her as a dominatrix he could still look at her as beneath him, regardless of the money she made, because he saw her work as demeaning. With Kelly being a lawyer or judge, things would be different. He was throwing a huge temper tantrum all about his own ego; instead of this being a cue for him to get off his ass and make something of his life, or at the least be proud of Kelly for taking action, he wanted to keep Kelly down with him.

He tried to continue the argument, but we tuned him out and talked about my trip. It became clear Kelly had moved past Drew and Drew was refusing to accept it. He became irate at being ignored. Finally, I couldn't keep my mouth shut.

"You are such a dick Drew. The only reason you're upset is because Kelly's achievements make your penis feel small. Go find someone less smart, less driven, and less powerful. I will not let you cut her down so you can feel better about yourself. Maybe it's time for you to take a long look in the mirror and get your lazy ass off of our fucking couch!"

I immediately regretted saying it, but I just got off a six-hour plane ride into this madness from my own week of drama, and I couldn't control myself.

Drew stared at Kelly, waiting for her to defend him. There was a long silence.

"You heard the girl, bitch!" she said to him firmly.

And that was the end of Kelly and Drew.

Wow, it is so much easier to break up with someone else's boyfriend. I had wanted to tell Drew off for a while, ever since the mooching became blatantly obvious.

Kelly wasn't that upset over Drew. She wasn't exactly monogamous, even though he assumed she was. He insisted no labels, but Kelly was the one who took advantage of it. She was excited to start fresh. We spent the rest of the night talking about what Kelly's new future would be like, the new circle of friends she would have, the types of clothes she would have to wear. It was fun picturing Kelly turning her life completely upside-down. Over the past few years she had become more like me...I was the one who was supposed to go to law school, according to my parents...and I was becoming more like her...a bohemian artist on the road to sexual freedom. We'd practically traded places.

It was almost October and the autumn chill was in the air. Kelly was out for dinner with some NYU friends that didn't drop out, who she stayed in touch with but rarely saw, so she didn't see me racing around the apartment nervously getting ready for the date she didn't know I had.

Peter picked me up at 7:00 p.m., kissed my cheek gently before we got in the Uber and headed over to a French place he loved on the Upper East Side, La Goulue. We sat at a romantic table in a nook by the window; he pulled my chair out for me as I sat down. I wasn't familiar with French food so I let him make suggestions. We shared a lovely evening and a delicious bottle of wine. Peter was a perfect gentleman, the food was scrumptious, and the conversation was the ideal mix of intellect and humor. We talked about our childhoods, our favorite music and our favorite things to do in the city. Peter told me about his passion for travel and how he had been on every continent. He reminded me of a younger, more serious version of Henry. They seemed to belong to the same wealthy social scene. But Henry was a big kid and a lot of fun, whereas Peter was more reserved. I was intrigued by him.

I was tipsy by the time dessert arrived at the table. I shuffled my chair to the other side of the table next to his.

"You've been so far away all night," I said as I leaned my head on his shoulder. I left my head resting there until the check came.

"I'm sorry, two cocktails and a bottle of wine is more than I can handle. They kept topping up my glass. I wasn't paying attention," I slurred, clutching Peter's arm.

"I'm sorry, I should have taken better care of you. What would you like to do now? Where can I take you?" he comforted me.

"Can we go home?" I asked as the world swirled around me.

"Sure." He kissed my forehead.

We got into a taxi and I immediately lay my head on his lap, slipping in and out of consciousness.

"We're here. Do you need help getting upstairs?" he asked.

"Where are we?" I asked with my head still on his lap.

"We're at your apartment. You said you wanted to go home," he explained.

"I meant your home…" I started laughing.

"Not tonight, darling," he said tenderly. "Would you like me to help you inside?"

I nodded.

Peter paid the taxi driver and then helped me up six flights of stairs. It was barely ten p.m. "I'm sorry I ruined your night." I fumbled to get my keys in the door.

He took them from my hand and opened the door.

"Don't be silly. I had a really nice time with you. Can we have brunch tomorrow? They have a great one near me on Columbus..." he said sweetly.

"Brunch? Don't you want to come in?" I slurred.

He kissed my forehead for like the fifth time that night and left. I quickly passed out on my bed in my clothes, shoes, and makeup.

My phone woke me up at 10:00 a.m. sharp. I was relieved I didn't have a hangover. I met Peter at a great cafe around the corner from his apartment. He had a frittata and I French toast. We both stayed away from the mimosas. He got extra points for being a gentleman the night before and not taking advantage of how drunk I was.

After brunch, we walked around the Upper West Side to check out a street fair. On the weekends in Manhattan while the weather was nice they close down about ten blocks on a random street every weekend and set up kiosks with vendors selling everything from socks, pillows and Japanese tea sets to jewelry, roasted corn on the cob, and back massages...you name it, they probably have it. It was a mild day, the sun was shining, and the streets were crowded.

We walked around for hours, talking about our lives. Peter told me about his work. I told him about the theater company in the Village and my job with Henry. We really hit it off. Peter bought me a photograph of Central Park and bought us each a ten-minute massage in a tent, which was fun.

After the fair he invited me back to his place to cook dinner with him. He lived in a beautiful two-bedroom apartment on Central Park West right along the park. He had a grand piano in his living room; that was the first thing I noticed. I was curious.

"That's a beautiful piano, do you play?" I asked.

"Since I was seven. I used to play concerts all through high school but I got nervous in front of a crowd; it took all the joy away, so I just play for myself now. It's kind of my sanity."

There were large leather couches in the living room and lots of eclectic art collected during Peter's travels across the globe. They didn't necessarily match the rest of the décor, but it gave the place a cosmopolitan feel.

"I bought some salmon at the market this morning; I hope that's alright," he said as he headed into the kitchen.

"Sounds great," I followed him like an eager puppy. "What are we making?" I flirted.

He smiled. "Grilled salmon, steamed spinach and kale, with a little penne vodka on the side."

"Oooo, sounds yummy."

I was Peter's helper in the kitchen, doing my best to keep my mouth shut and not take over—I couldn't help but get a little bossy in the kitchen and, after all, it wasn't my kitchen. I cleaned and cut the veggies, but Peter did all the real cooking. It was fun. I loved that he knew how to cook, and clean up when he was done. I knew it was silly, but after living with Russell, a man who could clean up after himself was a big turn on.

Dinner was delicious, the food and the company. Peter was so smart and could talk about anything. I enjoyed learning from him and was interested in what he had to say about everything from investments to politics and world issues. We ended up on his huge, comfy leather couch after dinner and snuggled up to an old movie playing on AMC. I was getting a little antsy. He still hadn't kissed me. Was this guy going to make a move, or what?

His arm was around me and my head was resting on his shoulder. Maybe this was too awkward a position for him to kiss me, so I readjusted. No luck. Then it occurred to me: maybe he was looking for a girl he wanted to actually spend time with, not just screw around with. Just as that thought was formulating in my head, I felt Peter's lips brush against my cheek. I looked up at him and his lips met mine.

It was a deep, long kiss. There was nothing hasty about it; it didn't feel like it was a kiss to pave the way to more fondling. It was kissing as an art form. Kissing as an act of intense pleasure in itself. Like the way kissing used to feel before I started doing all the other stuff that kissing opened the door to. We must have made out for an hour. I was draped across his lap on the couch as he held me in his arms. I was so aroused I was sweating.

He stopped. "Would you like some tea or dessert?"

"I would love some tea." He went into the kitchen and I slouched down on the couch until he returned with two mugs. He set them down on coasters on the coffee table. He returned next to me, lifted me back on his lap and we resumed kissing. His hands wandered up my sweater and over my bra. He pulled my sweater off over my head and I was left in a tank top. He unsnapped the clasp on my bra and took it off with the tank top in one motion. His hands wandered over my breasts as our lips were locked. He gently teased my nipples and tickled my stomach. He touched my nipples in a way that I could feel between my legs. Each time he caressed my nipple it was as if he was massaging my clitoris. I had no idea my nipples were connected to my vagina. I could have sworn he gave me an orgasm just from massaging my breasts. Is there even such thing as a nipple-gasm?

My body was writhing, my ass grinding on his lap, and I felt him grow hard under me. With every touch he sent my body into an uncontrollable frenzy. After another hour of Peter teasing me it was time for me to get home. Monday was going to be a challenge, catching up on everything I missed at work when I was in LA. I pulled myself away from his lips while his hands were still tweaking my nipples.

"I have to get going ..." Peter interrupted me with another kiss.

He held me on his lap for a few moments; it was close to eleven o'clock.

"I had a great time with you today," he said.

"Me too," I beamed.

We kissed once more passionately and I put my bra, tank top, and sweater back on. He called me an Uber and walked me down when it arrived.

"I look forward to seeing you again," he said as he closed the Uber door.

I was meditating on the sensation of him touching me the entire car ride home. I wasn't sure if I was more impressed with his boob fondling skills or that fact that he didn't try to go any further. I couldn't wait to see him again. I wasn't getting ahead of myself; I was just along for the ride. I wasn't looking at him as my future, just that he could be Mr. Right Now...an intelligent, sophisticated guy; someone I could learn a few things from. I enjoyed his company and thought the sex might be really good if we ever got there. Hanging with Peter could be fun and casual, but I wasn't about to fall for this guy or anything...

That following week life was back to normal at work with Henry and I started rehearsals for the play I landed during the summer. The production was to open in January. It was an important and provocative new drama by an up-and-coming playwright performing Off-Broadway at the SoHo Playhouse. I was playing the female lead with some heavy scenes, including an on-stage rape scene. I had my work cut out for me. It was hard to focus; I was happy, truly happy and I didn't want to go to a dark place in my spare time. My mind kept wandering towards my romance with Peter.

By the end of October, I was totally falling for Peter. In just a few weeks he had completely swept me off my feet. The New York

Philharmonic, The Public Theater, the Knicks…He was so attentive and considerate and sophisticated. I felt protected and cared for. He was chivalrous; he would open doors for me, pull out my chair, always paid for my car ride home so I wouldn't take the train late at night. As much as I loved my independence, it felt really nice to be treated so tenderly. At times, he was a little patronizing or condescending towards me, but he had a decade of experience and world-travel on me. I couldn't disrespect that. He was also a closet virtuoso on the piano. Sometimes affluence comes with a smidge of arrogance and the overprotection felt romantic.

It was convenient that rehearsals kept me busy, I wasn't able to get too needy and it made things clear to Peter that I had a full and exciting life outside of dating him. The first few dates were all about me in the pleasure department. Peter insisted on taking care of me and refused to let me reciprocate. Initially I was suspicious if he had issues in that department. I couldn't understand it. It's close to never that you meet a guy who doesn't want his dick sucked. He turned me down on three different occasions when I hinted at going further. I speculated that maybe he had herpes or a weird birthmark on it or some other STD; my mind was racing with so many different scenarios that could justify this strange behavior. It was driving me crazy. After our fifth date, three weeks in, he asked me to be exclusive. Then he finally let me take his pants off and to my surprise and delight he had a very handsome sidekick in full working order.

In the past guys would try to coerce me to have sex with them early on with no commitment, it was the opposite with Peter. Even once his pants came off, he still wasn't pushing to go all the way with me. We fooled around for several weeks before he took me. I became comfortable lounging around his apartment naked with him; whether we were cooking, reading, or watching TV, we were always naked. We were even naked when he played the piano and I massaged his shoulders. He had a husky body, but was a runner and did five miles in the park every morning. By the time we did the deed he knew every inch of my body and what buttons to push. We had many marathon sessions exploring each other's erogenous zones before we fucked. Peter didn't just want to have sex with me; he wanted me to *need it*, to *crave him*…he wanted me begging for it before he gave it to me, and that's exactly what I did.

Precisely one month after our first date we were lying on the rug next to the grand piano; he was playing a symphony on my body, our skin was moist, and I found myself begging for it. "I need you inside of me right now, I can't take it anymore."

He continued teasing me. I grabbed his shoulder, digging my nails into his skin just enough to scratch the surface. I needed him to know I was serious.

"I need you to fuck me right now, or I'm leaving!" I threatened.

"Oh really, you want it that bad?" he teased.

"I'm serious, what do I have to do to make you give it to me? Do I have to beg you for it?" I groaned rolling around the rug naked in blissful frustration.

Peter slid me off of him, stood up, and walked down the hall.

"Where are you going?" I fumed naked on the rug.

He slowly sauntered to the bathroom and returned with a condom.

"I thought you wanted to get fucked!" he said as he tossed the wrapper aside and rolled the condom on himself.

"Where do you want me?" I asked rolling around breathless with desire.

"Right there," he said as he got on the floor and climbed over me.

"Are you sure you want my cock? I'm only gonna give it to you if you really want it." I was squirming beneath him gyrating my hips trying to meet him with my pelvis, nodding my head. He slid himself against my lower lips, teasing me slowly.

"I want it so bad," I whispered, my eyes locked with his.

"You'll get it, soon, very soon."

He continued rubbing against me, getting slippery with my excitement. He guided himself into me slowly, inching his way in and pulling back each time I tried to push up against him, to take him deeper. My legs open to capacity, pelvis reached towards him, my whole body arched and finally he gave himself to me, entirely. As our flesh tangled together Peter enveloped me in his arms and rolled me over so I was on top of him. He slowly guided my hips in a circular motion gliding me along his pelvic bone as he penetrated me, working his way in deeper and deeper with my breasts against his chest. His big hands moved my body freely, speeding up the motion, sending earthquakes through me until I shot up, upright on his cock and my entire body shook out of control on top of him. I could feel him pulsing and releasing inside of me.

He grinned at the scale of my orgasm, proud of himself; it was epic. I was kinda embarrassed; I had never lost control like that before. I flopped off of him and collapsed on the rug beside him. He kissed my forehead, rolled off the filled condom and tossed it to the side.

I learned with Peter that a proper orgasm should render one entirely useless. He left me sprawled across the rug, exhausted after we arrived. He got up and sat down at the grand piano and played, as I lay naked beneath it. I could feel the vibrations of the music reverberate through my body. With each note I could feel aftershocks of pleasure surge through my insides. I couldn't stand up or string a sentence together. Peter looked down at me with an evil grin on his face.

"You asked for it," he reminded me as he fingered the keys.

He gave me orgasms that sent me to the moon before he would even get to my vagina. I learned a lot from Peter, mostly about myself. He was sensual and erotic. He liked to take his time and savor the pleasure moments. Most of the sex I had before seemed rushed in comparison. He gave me wonderful long massages and found different ways to arouse me. He taught me what he liked and how to please him. I was happy to learn, to reciprocate, to be able to give him back some of the pleasure he gave me.

Could this be it? Could he be *the one*? I didn't think I was ready to settle down so soon but I could really see a future with Peter. I'd had my fun; I'd slept with five guys since Russell, fooled around with a few others and made out with two girls. Was that enough? Or did the right person fill in the gaps and make it enough?

NOV | FUCKED

"What if I made a mistake?" I asked Kelly as my heart sank.

"If it doesn't feel right, don't do it. Period!" she said as she gave me a reassuring look and hugged me tight.

I was crazy for Peter within a month. He was worldly, caring, and intelligent. And the sex! God, the sex was intense. Is there such a thing as too many orgasms? Kelly didn't think so. He exposed me to so many new ideas in and out of the bedroom. He had impeccable taste, interesting friends, and was an amazing cook. He was also a successful businessman, so I really looked up to him. I was caught up in the bliss.

We were spending weekend getaways with his friends, who were a combination of executives and accomplished creative types. He received too many social invitations to keep up with them all. I was just happy to be along for the ride. I was exposed to a new social network. His friends were polite and did their best to make me feel welcome. Once they were able to get to know me, they all seemed to like me, but it was hard to tell. I could sense some of the women sizing me up a bit, but I was confident enough to handle it. My boss, Henry, was a popular and controversial name among the New York elite, but I never talked about my job. I chose to talk about the play I was working on instead. I was really proud of it.

We were in the Hamptons for a weekend in November when I ran into Henry at an afternoon party. He was still playing the field since the model dumped him five months before and it was the longest I'd ever seen him without a girlfriend. He was flirting with a group of socialite types when I noticed him across the room.

"Hey, boss."

He was surprised to see me. I wasn't sure if he was surprised to see me in his social circle, or surprised because I caught him trying to pick up three girls at once.

"Dana, what are you doing here? I didn't know you came to the Hamptons." He gave me a tender hug, almost forgetting he was in mid-conversations with three Scandinavian beauties.

"I'm here with my boyfriend, Peter."

"Does he have a place out here?" Henry asked.

"His parents do, but we're staying with some friends," I stated.

He looked me up and down slowly. I was wearing a turquoise bandage dress and black stilettos. The dress was a gift from Peter. We chatted for a few minutes before Peter spotted me from across the room. He saw me giggling and smiling with Henry and made a beeline over to us. Sometimes men are so predictable. I was pleased with his reaction; I wanted it to be clear to him I was desirable, and desired by others. In that moment, I wanted him to know that I had many options, even if I didn't exactly believe it myself.

"Hey," Peter said as he approached me from behind, wrapped his arms around my waist and kissed my neck. "I've been looking for you."

I gently slipped out of his grasp. I could instantly feel tension among the three of us. "Peter, this is Henry, my boss." I said as I smiled awkwardly.

"Henry, this is Peter." They both forced smiles at each other.

There was a long pause.

"I'm going to get a drink. It was nice running into you, Henry." I leaned in and kissed him on the cheek.

"Nice to meet you," Peter said, shaking his hand stiffly.

Henry glared at us as we walked away. Ever since his birthday, things with Henry had been a little weird, but we did our best to pretend things were normal. Neither of us ever talked about what happened that night, the kiss, anything. Henry had been looking at me differently ever since. If he wasn't my boss, I would have for sure dated him. Well, if I wasn't with Peter. I was sure Henry understood that I cherished my job; he was awesome to work for, was totally flexible when I needed him to be, appreciated me, and paid me really well. There were also a ton of perks, like red carpet events and free lunches and dinners at places I wasn't prepared to splurge on. I was very fond of him, but I also knew what kind of a player he was. It was hard to keep Henry interested in anything for too long.

Peter was passive-aggressive with me the rest of the afternoon. He barely said two words to me. Finally, when we went back to the house where we were staying to change before dinner, he started with the interrogation.

"How long have you been working for him? Do you flirt with him all the time? Have you ever been involved?"

I did my best to reassure Peter that Henry was just my boss and a friend, that I worked for him for many years and we had been there for each other through some rough times, but no, we'd never been involved. I didn't tell him about the birthday kiss; he would have taken it all out of context and the weekend would have been ruined.

"You are the only one I want to be with; I don't care what else is out there. Nobody has ever made me feel the way you do," I said as I pressed my body up against Peter's and kissed his neck ever so softly.

Work and rehearsals were keeping me away from Peter more than he liked as the holiday season was creeping up on us. Peter picked me up from rehearsal one night when I was running behind. He quickly noticed it was only two of us actors and the male director at the theater that late. The other cast members were let go once they finished their scenes and the stage manager had to cut out early. The rest of us were in the middle of a heavy scene and eager to get through it. It was a steamy love scene. The chemistry between Marcus and I was undeniable as we shouted at each other across the stage. Inching closer together, softening as our bodies drew in like magnets, slowly avoiding the pull unsuccessfully. Then suddenly Marcus grabbed me to kiss me, our faces were barely touching…

"Nice, work!" The director, Erez, applauded from his seat before we got to the kiss. Marcus and I both looked out at the audience, breathless, and were encouraged by the director's approval.

After that night, picking me up from rehearsals became a regular thing for Peter. He would always treat me to dinner and escort me home after, even if I didn't spend the night with him. Between meeting Henry and catching glimpses of my rehearsals, Peter was keen on discussing our future together. It had barely been two months but he was eager to talk about the big picture of where this relationship was going.

Could this be it? Could Peter be *the one*? Sure, my mind drifted off into fantasyland from time to time, daydreaming about playing house with him on Central Park West, but was I ready? Was he what I wanted? How long does it take to know? How would I know? I started wondering why he was still single. How did he not have a girlfriend or a wife already? He was already in his mid-thirties, an incredible boyfriend and a major catch. I didn't get the Henry playboy vibe from him at all. According to Peter he was busy travelling and establishing his career, but *now* it was time to get serious. He genuinely wanted to settle down and have a family before forty, and that was fast approaching. His words, not mine.

Life with him was like a dream; he took care of everything. He even took me to Europe for a week over Thanksgiving. He surprised me with tickets after I told him I had never been. We visited London and Paris.

In London, we stayed at a boutique hotel in Chelsea and spent our first day wandering around the expensive shops. The next day we went for breakfast, then shopping at Harrods and each bought a pair of shoes. We caught a matinee at the Globe Theatre and walked along the Thames. We had dinner and drinks on the top of the Shard overlooking the entire city. It was mild for the end of November and we walked almost everywhere, stumbling upon different pockets of town and unique shops. The city felt electric and Peter relished my childlike excitement.

Next, we headed to Paris and stayed at the opulent Four Seasons hotel off the Champs-Élysées. We walked the streets, popping in and out of small boutiques. We enjoyed pastries and delectable sweets, spent an entire day in the Louvre, sipped cappuccino in cafes, and dined in bistros. He spoiled me on the trip with shopping, insisting I couldn't go all the way to Paris without getting a few outfits. I had some of the best food on the planet; it was the most incredible adventure of my life. At the top of the Eiffel Tower he told me he loved me for the first time. We kissed in the sky overlooking Paris for what seemed like forever.

When we returned to the hotel that night the room was filled with white roses and a bottle of Dom Perignon chilling on a cart with fresh fruit and sweets. He popped open the bottle of champagne and poured us each a glass. But before he let me have a sip, he revealed a small velvet box from his pocket and slowly lowered onto one knee. He proposed to me with his grandmother's antique ring, an art deco

European cut diamond adorned with diamonds and sapphires along the sides. It was breathtaking. My eyes filled with tears and I was so overwhelmed with emotion that I could barely squeak out the word, "Yes."

I felt like Cinderella or Pretty Woman or something. I was head over heels in love and so was he. Everything in my life was finally coming together. I wasn't looking for forever when I started seeing Peter, but I could definitely picture my future with him.

As soon as we returned to New York and I walked into my apartment in Hell's Kitchen I was uneasy. Kelly leapt out of her room to hear all about the trip.

"So, miss jetsetter, how was Paris?" she inquired while my bags were still in hand.

I dropped my carry-on and extended my left arm to show her the antique 2.5-karat rock.

"Holy fuck! You're engaged?"

"Uh-huh," I nodded, unsure.

"How did this happen?"

"I'm not sure, it all happened so fast." I shrugged.

"You think? You've only known him a couple of months." Kelly was as confused about the situation as I was.

"We were in Paris and it was so romantic and he spoiled me like crazy," I defended.

"That's all great, but do you even want to get married, like, now, like to Peter?" she continued.

"He is handsome and successful and treats me better than anyone I've ever been with."

"That wasn't the question, do you want to get married NOW?" she pressed.

"Maybe. I know it's fast, but he loves me, he really does."

"So what? You haven't been together long enough to see what he's like when things get challenging. It's all been champagne and caviar. You haven't even met his family. He hasn't been to Canada to meet yours. If this is what you want, I will be happy for you, but what's the rush…for him? I can't help but be a little suspicious."

Kelly was the voice of reason. In my gut things didn't feel right when he proposed, but I was so eager to please my Prince Charming I hesitated expressing my concerns and just went along with it.

I was at work when I got the call. The call I had been dreading for years. I didn't pick up on time and there was a message on my phone from my mom, her voice shaking on the other end. I dropped the phone and burst into tears, collapsing onto the floor in Henry's office, sobbing. Sean had another cardiac arrest, his third one since he'd gone into a coma, four years prior. This time they couldn't resuscitate him.

Henry came running into his office to see what all the commotion was. I was curled up in a ball when Henry reached me. He knelt down by my side and held me.

"What is it, sweetie?" he asked me softly.

"Sean, the one in a coma…"

Henry comforted me as I cried all over his dress shirt, staining it with snot and mascara. He didn't say anything. He just sat on the floor of his office with me for a good ten minutes while I sobbed in his arms.

When I finally pulled myself together, I looked up at Henry. "I have to go; the funeral is tomorrow. I'll be gone about a week."

Henry nodded. "Is there anything I can do?"

"You already did it," I told him and gathered my things. Henry kissed me on the forehead and I headed home.

I called my mother as I walked out of the office. She was crying on the other end. She was already online looking for a flight to get me home that night, but no luck. The funeral was the next day at 10:00 a.m. I quickly booked a bus ticket. It was a thirteen-hour bus ride overnight, departing from Port Authority at 7:00 p.m., arriving in Toronto at 8:00 a.m. the following morning.

I rushed back to my apartment. I tore through my room and threw clothing from my shelves in anger, shattering a small mirror and a jewelry box. I collapsed on the bed and wept. There were no words to describe the loss. I felt like a huge part of myself was gone, evaporated, vanished. The pain was paralyzing. I couldn't believe that I would never see Sean again, never laugh with him, or make movies with him.

Five years before, all I'd wanted was to get to New York to *start my life*. I'd abandoned him in a hospital in Canada. Now, I would have given it all back just to hear his voice again. I would have traded everything I had ever done in New York to make him well. I would have never moved away if I knew he wouldn't make it out of the hospital. I felt so terribly guilty for leaving him when he was ill.

It was almost four o'clock when Kelly got home and entered the disaster area that was my room.

"Wow, girl. Whatever you lost, you ain't gonna to find it in this mess…" She then noticed my red, puffy, and swollen face in mid-sentence and could tell something was terribly wrong. "What happened?"

I tried to tell her, but I couldn't get the words out, I sobbed again and fell onto the bed. Kelly came and sat next to me and put her hand on my back. "It's okay, cry it out. Let it all out."

I sat up and hugged her tight. I whispered in her ear, "Sean died today." Kelly held me as I cried in her arms.

"I really miss him. I haven't had him to talk to in so long. Before I moved to New York we barely went a day without talking or seeing each other since we were eight. He is a part of me and I can't believe he's gone," I screeched.

"He will always be a part of you," Kelly said as she held me tight until, eventually exhausted, I stopped weeping.

Kelly helped me pack my suitcase and put my room back together before we headed to the bus station. She came with me in the cab and waited at the terminal until I boarded the bus. I felt like a zombie, disconnected from my body and my emotions. I had gone numb. I finally remembered to call Peter and let him know what happened. He offered to meet me in Canada, but I refused. It wasn't the right time to bring him home. I wanted to honor Sean's memory, not flaunt my new fancy fiancé. The bus was full when I boarded and emptied at a constant pace, as we made our way north toward the Adirondacks. I stared out the window into the dark night; I couldn't see much, just shadows. Nothing made sense. Sean was like a compass that gave my life direction; without him I was lost. I didn't even know who I was. All of the talent and confidence I possessed was because he recognized those things in me. Without his belief in me, I didn't believe in myself.

My memories of Sean played on a loop in my head the entire ride to Toronto. I didn't sleep. My mind was racing. All these memories of my childhood, grade school, and high school kept flooding my mind. Sean's face, his smile, his laughter kept repeating on auto-play in my head.

My parents picked me up at the bus station in downtown Toronto at 8:00 a.m. on a Tuesday. We drove home so I could change, but there was no time to shower; home was nearly two hours away from the bus station.

Sean had been part of the family for almost two decades. Growing up, we practically lived at each other's houses, and my whole family (myself included) expected us to end up together...until he came out.

The funeral hall was packed; all the seats were filled and there were over thirty people standing in the back of the room. There were all the kids from high school I hadn't seen in years and the crowd from the Gayborhood, Sean's family, our neighbors...it seemed like the entire town was there. His brother spoke beautifully. Eloquent. Profound. He did Sean's memory justice in his passionate account of Sean's character. The room wept.

After the service, we proceeded to the cemetery. Everyone kept telling me how sorry they were, they knew how close we were, was I doing okay? Why were they sorry for me? Sean was the one I was sorry for, for all the things he would never have a chance to experience, the films he'd never get to make, the life he'd never get to live, the person he'd never get to be, stuck at twenty-five forever. I wept for his brilliance and for him never having a chance to share it with the world. I wept for all the moments in my life I imagined him being there for and now would miss out on.

It was a sunny brisk day and a sea of suits crowded around Sean's grave. I remember flashes: my parents standing on either side of me, holding my hands. His mother's face. My grandmother handing me tissues. People taking turns shoveling dirt onto the grave. I stayed and waited. When the grave was filled with dirt, people filtered off to pay their condolences at his parents' house following the funeral. I stood there. As the crowd dissipated, Chris found me and we embraced and wept at the graveside. I told my parents I would get a lift back with him and that I needed a few moments alone. I stood there under the cold sun, my face covered in tears and snot. I wished I could trade places with him. He deserved to live so much more than me; he had so much more to offer the world. I sat in the dirt next to his grave and patted the earth that covered where his casket was buried.

"I never stopped loving you. You are forever in my heart and in my thoughts and I am so pissed off at you for leaving me."

I kissed my hand and patted the dirt sitting there in a daze. I was drained and filthy, and I couldn't pull myself away.

"It's time to go, love; I'll come back with you tomorrow," Chris said as he helped me to stand. Chris was calmer than I expected him to be. I was almost angry with him not being more emotional, but I reminded myself that people grieve differently. I also remembered that Chris was the one who stayed by Sean's bedside and I was the one who left. I wasn't there with him every week in the hospital for five years. Chris was stoic and supportive. His love for Sean never wavered, even when he eventually dated other people. Chris must have felt a huge relief that he wouldn't have to spend any more nights in a horrible place watching his love literally fade away.

Chris drove me home.

"I was a terrible friend," I said as I started crying again. "I should have never left when he was sick."

"Don't do that. Sean was so proud of you. You being in New York is what kept him going a lot of the time. He loved when I read your letters about the theater company and Kelly and how exciting the city was. It kept him fighting, knowing that you were forging ahead with his mission. To him you being there meant a piece of him was there, too. He would have been so pissed if you squashed your talent and stayed home wasting your life becoming another boring person that he couldn't stand. Before the coma, he told me all the time about how you were his star and he had all the faith in the world that you would make it."

We got to my parents' house and I took a quick shower and changed my clothes. My mom gave us some tea while she told the story about the time Sean and I were playing in the backyard and got caught showing each other our business. We were forbidden to play together after that, but we both cried every night after school so the separation only lasted four days.

Chris and I walked across the street to Sean's parents' house, which was full of people. A group of our friends sat with Sean's father in the living room recounting stories from high school and childhood. We spent hours reminiscing over inside jokes and embarrassing moments. Like the time in high school we snuck into a Goth club, on Queen Street West and Sean volunteered for a contest where he had to lick chocolate pudding off of a stranger in lingerie. Or the time we went to an open mic at a dive bar in Parkdale full of shady weirdos and druggies. In high school, he always sought out alternative adventures, and like a puppy, I always followed along.

Chris and I tidied up the kitchen and the dining room. We washed dishes, transferred the food from catering trays to Tupperware, and wiped down the floors and countertops.

Sean's mother poked her head in the kitchen. "Thank you for cleaning up, and for today, for all those stories. I was hoping you might be able to get your friends back on the weekend, so I can record some of those anecdotes and memories. I'm getting older and I know I'll forget them. And I don't want to forget them," she said as tears filled her eyes.

Chris and I nodded.

I went up to Sean's room when we finished cleaning up. It was exactly the same as it was before he went in the hospital. There was not a single piece of white showing through the walls; they were covered in movie posters and magazine cutouts of actors and musicians he admired. He had notebooks of his writing on his desk, and a huge floor-to-ceiling bookshelf full of books and DVDs. I opened his closet and smelled his clothes. I missed his smell, his real smell, not the smell that was on him in the hospital. I found the second-hand Gucci suit he wore to prom, laid it on the bed and curled up next to it. All I'd wanted for the past year was just to have a conversation with him, to share all the crazy shit I'd done, mostly to impress him. Also, because he had been my best friend my whole life, if I wasn't telling Sean about my life it was hard to feel like myself.

Lying on his bed, I remembered the last thing he said to me at the hospital a few weeks before he went into a coma … I was gushing about Russell and how his band was starting to get momentum…

~ ~ ~ ~ ~

"He sounds like a total loser," Sean mumbled. "And he's totally in the way of why you went to New York in the first place."

I couldn't understand why Sean was so upset about my relationship with Russell. He found a partner, Chris, and was happy. Didn't I deserve someone?

As I wheeled Sean back to his room, Chris was there waiting with some takeout. Chris helped Sean back in the bed and, after a few moments of chatting, I left them to their dinner.

"I love you with all my heart. Keep fighting. You're gonna get out soon," I whispered into his ear while holding him tight.

"I'm totally pissed off at you. You've been in New York well over a year and you've been to more of Russell's shows than auditions," he whispered in my ear.

I stepped back and looked at him. I tried not to let the words sting, but they did.

"You have way too much talent to waste your life being some fucking groupie!"

~ ~ ~ ~ ~

While all the movie stars and creative geniuses that papered his bedroom walls were staring down at me, I vowed to make all of our dreams reality. Sean never got the opportunity to become a filmmaker or go after his dreams, but I was lucky enough to be alive and have my health, so I would live our dreams for the both of us.

After the funeral, I returned to New York with an overwhelming drive to succeed…not only at my career, but at life. And *living* it the way *I* wanted.

Now back in New York I couldn't deny my true feelings. When I voiced my concerns about us rushing into marriage, Peter got defensive. When I suggested we slow down a bit and put the engagement on hold for a few months until we met each other's families, he became agitated and insisted we would not go backwards. I felt a little trapped, I loved him and wanted to stay with him, but I really wasn't ready to be engaged.

The more *he* discussed our future plans, the more I realized how much my life would change being Peter's wife. Come the new year he insisted I leave my job with Henry, that he would find me a suitable position at his family's company where I would remain until we started our own family, then, of course, I would be at home taking care of our minimum of three children. I would have the option of returning to work at the company part-time once the kids were in school full-time. He would *allow* me to keep writing as a creative outlet, but this play would be my last acting role; he would not allow *his wife* and mother of *his children* to be out late at rehearsals doing love scenes with random men.

When I tried to express how important my creative work was, he scolded me "Dana, it's time to grow up and stop living in your fantasy world. The life I can give is better than you could ever do on your own, or with anyone else. What's the problem?" He couldn't fathom that I could want anything beyond what he could provide for me.

I was crushed. How much of myself would I have to give up to be with him? I didn't know what had happened, but once he put that ring on my finger it was clear he saw me as his property, not a person.

I wandered home from his apartment along the park in the 80s to my place in Hell's Kitchen in the late 40s that cold night. Icy tears streamed down my face as I contemplated my future with and without Peter. Staying with him, my life would be set. I wouldn't have to worry about income or work and I would have a pretty amazing jet-setting lifestyle. But it would all come at the cost of losing not only my freedom, but also the essence of myself. As I rounded the corner onto my block, Sean's words resonated in my memory: 'you have too much talent to waste your life being someone's groupie.' He was right. Staying with Peter would be me compromising my dreams for a man all over again. It would be my surrender. It would be me never realizing what I truly had inside myself. I wasn't ready to give up on *me* just yet.

I had no choice but to end it.

I dragged my feet up the never-ending flights of stairs to the apartment. I crept in quietly and knocked on Kelly's door.

"What's up Dana?"

I opened her door and sat on the bed as she dog-eared a corner of the book she was reading and set it on the nightstand.

My heart sank. "What if I made a huge mistake?" I asked softly.

"If it doesn't feel right, don't do it. Period!" She opened her arms and I fell into her embrace.

"I made a huge mistake; I haven't even told my parents yet," I sniffled into her shoulder.

"You're gonna be fine. Just tell Peter the truth and give him his grandma's ring back. He'll probably never talk to you again, but you will be fine."

I was covered in snot for days. Literally covered. You know when you cry so hard and so much there is not enough tissue in the world to contain the snot, so then you start using your shirt sleeve, and move on to your pant leg as the sleeves are too soggy and then eventually the sheet you have wrapped around you, because you are too weak and fragile to face the world and emerge from the cocoon, that the sheet itself turns into a gigantic bed-sheet sized tissue?

Between Sean and Peter, it was too much loss in a short amount of time. I felt so alone. The worst part was that I hadn't even been looking for anything serious. I was just having fun. Peter was the one who pushed for a commitment, a relationship, and marriage so fast my head was spinning.

I was so angry with myself for getting swept up in his charm, but I was also proud of myself for getting out and staying true to who I was.

There was nothing I could do…but write. I had a new fire in me, a new voice pouring out onto the pages, and a new power in my work. Rehearsals really started to spark once I was able to pull it together. Instead of letting the grief and heartbreak ruin me, I channeled my pain into making something memorable from it.

DEC | QUEER COMES THE BRIDE

"Who the hell are you? And what have you done with Kelly?"

I demanded answers from the woman standing in my living room.

I tried to enjoy my time off for the holidays in New York, but I couldn't help second-guessing my decision to end things with Peter. I got used to him taking care of me; it felt really good. I felt so stupid walking away from everything he was willing to give me. Would I ever find a guy like that again? Was I the one being unreasonable? I kept reminding myself what I would lose becoming his wife/prisoner… everything that made me *me*. Deep down I knew I was worth more than expensive gifts and trips around the world. I had no choice but to walk away. I owed it to Sean and to myself to find out what I was actually made of.

Over the break, Kelly and I took random dance and fitness classes in an effort not to couch-potato away our vacation time. Kelly was gearing up for her return to NYU to complete a few credits before starting law school in the fall and Henry was off to some exotic location with his newest flame, so I had time off from him and rehearsals.

I was done: with men…with sex…with love…for now…until I figured out what I really needed.

I was grateful that I had the play to focus on. Even though we had a break over the holidays, I worked on my lines and my role each day. The play was opening mid-January and I was determined to give it everything I had, for Sean. And for myself. As I thought about the acting work, I realized I was so close to giving up my passion for a relationship, again. I hadn't been going on auditions much while dating Peter. Sure, I'd been in rehearsals for a play, but I'd gotten that part back in June and I hadn't made an effort to find my next role. I planned to hit the ground running when I returned from LA, but all those plans went out the window once Prince Charming came along. In the midst of all his temptation I was able to find the courage to stand up for myself, finally. I was proud of my decision. It was time to focus and get serious.

"Don't be so hard on yourself, girl. Living life isn't just about work. Falling in love, gettin' your heart broken, breakin' some hearts, that's all part of it. You need all these experiences to make you a *person*. And as an artist it can give you more depth and provide you with some good material to write about."

Kelly always said the right things. She was much stronger than I was. She never let her value be defined by a man's interest in her. I wanted to be like that. She would never let a guy stand between her and her goals. When Drew was upset about her going to law school, she tossed him to the curb and never looked back. I wanted that confidence. I wanted to live my life not caring about other people's opinions of me. I wanted to be as strong as she was.

After Kelly's dad left, her mom was a mess. Alone with three kids to take care of and no education, she went from one relationship to another, totally dependent on a man's support both emotionally and financially. Kelly resolved in junior high that she would never rely on a man for anything (hence the three vibrators) and that her worth would never be defined by one, either.

Unlike Kelly, my self-esteem was linked to whether or not a guy was interested in me. First it was Sean who gave me my confidence, until he rejected me. Although we were never involved sexually, he would call me 'beautiful' and his 'muse', and that made me feel worthwhile. Then Russell, Trevor, Tony, Santiago, Josh and finally Peter. Looking back at the past year I could see how much energy I put into finding and pleasing guys. Why did I need a man to be interested in me to feel good about myself?

Kelly never waited to be picked. She didn't believe any of the stupid rules, so she didn't subscribe to them. She picked the guys. She was never afraid to make a move or take what she wanted. When Kelly mentioned the *Year of the Slut,* she wasn't telling me to be a slut—well she was, but not the way I thought. Kelly reclaimed the world *slut* as empowering. To her, it meant a strong, independent woman who had sex on her own terms, not that of society or, more accurately, men. In the past a slut would have been considered a woman who was insecure and desperate for the attention of men. Kelly redefined the word slut to mean a woman who determines her own worth and embraces her sexual power instead of feeling ashamed of it. Kelly didn't have sex to please a man; she had sex to please herself. It feels good to feel sexy and desired and to get a man's attention. Whether it leads to sex or not, there is excitement in flirtation alone. During my *Year of the Slut* I'd learned that sexual spark fuels me. I definitely had more confidence and drive when I felt sexy; it made me feel more powerful, too.

After Christmas, Kelly put the whole school mode into overdrive and decided it was time to reinvent herself. She decided to keep a few key clients for financial support through school, but, for the most part, she was leaving the dominatrix chapter of her life and the dungeon behind.

Kelly cleaned out her room, converting it to her new study space. She got rid of most of the art supplies and spools of material. She cleaned out her closet and donated a third of her clothing to Goodwill, bought a few bookcases to organize the stacks and stacks of books covering the floor. While Kelly was at it, I decided to clean out my room too. I have a theory that if you want to invite new things into your life you have to make room by getting rid of some old things. It was a great catharsis for both of us.

The next step was to get Kelly an appropriate law school wardrobe. Most of her stuff was outrageous or provocative and almost all second hand, except for her work attire; most of those get-ups were custom-made by Ricky. I was thrilled to get Kelly some actual new clothes, not something new that had been sitting at the second-hand shop for two years. We went to 34th Street to take advantage of the post-Christmas sales and traipsed through Macy's and a number of shops along the strip. I was a little surprised at the look she was going for. She took this whole reinvention thing to heart. We returned home with her new wardrobe of pencil skirts, slacks, blazers and button-down blouses all in neutral colors, gray, black and navy. She reasoned as long as she wore colorful naughty lingerie she wasn't completely selling out.

At home I made Kelly model all her new stuff and we put a few outfits together. Each time she looked in the mirror she would laugh and turn away and snap back all serious. "I look so weird in this."

Kelly had a full mane of curly red hair; it was long and wild and fit her personality perfectly.

"It's the hair. It doesn't go. No one will take me seriously with this hair."

"Don't say that! I love your hair. It's so long and beautiful and no one has that color naturally. It's you," I defended.

"You're right. It *is* me. The hair's definitely gotta go," she resolved.

The next day when I got home from work Kelly was glued to the mirror in the living room, staring at her new do.

"Who the hell are you? And what have you done with Kelly," I gasped.

She had chopped off all her luscious fiery locks and dyed it black. She looked strikingly beautiful and like someone you didn't want to mess with. I think it was the perfect mix of what she was going for.

I was so proud of Kelly. She was making leaps and bounds towards her future. She had grown so much since I had met her and taught me so much about the type of woman I strived to be. When I first met Kelly, I thought that she was going to be the one to learn from me; about table manners and etiquette, which she did. She was much neater since meeting me and didn't eat with her fingers as much. She started going for regular manicures and facials. But, over the years of knowing Kelly I learned way more from her. I learned that manners, grooming, and keeping a tidy home have little to do with being a real woman. Thanks to Kelly's world colliding with mine, I was finally getting closer to becoming the woman I wanted to be.

Ricky and Steve got married. They had a small wedding for about thirty guests on a beach near Key West over New Year's. Ricky threw a New Year's Eve party every year for the past five years, so he had no worries about his close friends being available to make it. They rented an Airbnb. It was a huge six-bedroom mansion on two acres and it backed onto a private beach. The house was white and sleek with floor-to-ceiling windows. The property was equipped with a large swimming pool, tennis court, full fitness room, yoga studio and sprawling gardens. They set up several glamping tents sporadically around the property to accommodate everyone. The pool was accompanied by cabanas and lounges, a pool house with a full kitchen, bathroom and guesthouse off of the pool, which was acting as a honeymoon suite for the weekend. They hired staff to provide yoga classes, massages, tarot readings, and tantric meditation for their guests to enjoy a full five-star treatment.

The flight was easy from JFK and Kelly came as my date; I couldn't bear going to a wedding alone so soon after giving the ring back. At least it was a gay wedding; if I had to see a traditional bride walk down the aisle in a white dress, I would have gone catatonic. With Peter I thought I was getting closer to walking down that aisle and now it felt further away than ever, but I didn't regret my decision.

I was thrilled for Steve and Ricky. The festivities began on a Friday afternoon and went through Sunday night. The invitation said clothing optional so most of the guests were in beach-wear, swimsuits, sarongs, and there were also a few body painted nudies in the mix, which was one of the special activities they had arranged for the weekend. As the day turned to night, more guests shed their layers and opted to be painted.

The ceremony was the following day on the private beach overlooking the water. Ricky was adorned with a white orchid tiara, bracelets and anklets and Steve was wearing a purple orchid lei, and they both had white leather Speedos encrusted with rhinestones that Ricky designed especially for the day.

The grooms were not the only ones decked out for the occasion. Ricky, being a designer, *had* to style the wedding and, lucky for him, he had access to all he needed. Ricky brought two suitcases full of samples and old inventory from the shop: all black leather gear. He personally dressed everyone for the ceremony; it took almost three hours to style us all, but he was totally in his element. There were shirtless men in leather shorts and suspenders, bears in ass-less chaps, jock types in leather kilts commando. Ladies in leather minis, pasties and crotchless panties. Dom's, Daddies, Divas, Slaves, Subs and Sparkles. Kelly opted for black glitter pasties and leather booty shorts. I chose a leather bustier and black tutu with rhinestones disbursed in the tulle circa the Madonna *Like a Virgin* era. Aside from the two of us prudes, the guests were mostly half, if not fully, exposed. We were at a nude gay wedding on a beach at sunset on New Year's Eve. Wow! I reflected, "It really has been a slutty year."

In spite of the spectacle, the service was touching, and Ricky and Steve were emotional while exchanging their vows. After the ceremony ended the party got wild with a DJ spinning disco tunes and bubbly flowing. They built a bonfire in the fire pit and lit tiki torches lining the property and reflecting fire off the water. Dinner was catered and the party kept moving, from tent, to cabana, to house, to pool. It was a blast. After dinner the treats came out; in addition to the alcohol, Steve procured party favors for the guests, including coke and old school ecstasy.

Kelly and I needed to let loose. I was still recovering from my recent grief and breakup and Kelly had been working double time, eager to save up as much as she could before diving back into academia.

"I grabbed us some X." I grinned with wide eyes.

"I'm good, honey," Kelly said, shaking her head.

"Really? I thought for sure you'd want to get blasted one last time before school..."

Kelly wasn't interested in getting high. It had been months since she had been intoxicated...since that night we never talked about.

"Girl, if you're in the mood, go for it. You could use some fun. I'll make sure to keep you safe," she offered as she gave me a hug.

Safe? I thought to myself. Something definitely had changed. Now Kelly was the one being protective and I was seeking out the free drug buffet? I didn't think about it for too long and downed the small pill with champagne and led Kelly to the dance floor. We twirled to old school Madonna and Wham, singing all the words under our breath as we broke out the cheesiest moves we could remember from our childhood, which was still a decade later than those hits.

I walked towards the shore, the cool sand between my toes, and thought how Sean would have loved this kind of thing. It was the party of the year, for sure, maybe even the decade. The beach, the house, the costumes, the drugs. It was perfect; a perfect expression of *them*. I missed Peter and wished I wasn't alone. Not the overbearing dictator, the Prince Charming version of him that he was at the beginning. I also knew this was not his scene and that he would have been out of his mind judgmental. Come to think of it we really weren't that compatible in many ways. I wondered if I would ever find my perfect match. Then I remembered Ricky and Steve met at a gang bang. That made me re-think the whole concept of being open to the universe; things happen in their own time and when you least expect it. Before I could mope for too long the ecstasy crept up on me and I was drawn back to the music and flailing on the dance floor.

I had a group of half-naked men gathered around me, cheering me on as I danced.

"You go girl!" one shouted.

"Get down, you sexy thang!" another added.

They both grinded their hard bodies against me as we danced until my feet hurt. They spanked my ass and fondled my breasts and I welcomed it. My body was passed around the dance floor. Ricky and Steve resurfaced and joined the drug induced dancing orgy that broke out in their absence. Limbs and bodies gyrated and rolled off of and onto one another to the vibrations, hands exploring strangers. Many couples and groups broke off into rooms and tents as it got later. A bunch of us stayed outside until the sun came up. Some people took more drugs, trying to keep the high going; others, like me, were happy to come down as the sun came up.

A great party was just what the doctor ordered, but coming down off the ecstasy, watching the staff clean up the morning-after mess, was depressing, reminding me of how something so beautiful can end in ruin, like that night in the hotel with Russell when we trashed the room, or everything with Peter. Sitting on a lounge chair beside Kelly, looking out into the clear blue water of the pool, I pondered the amount of planning and hoping and money and effort that go into such a fleeting moment that's over so quickly. It then occurred to me, maybe that's what life is, fleeting moments…and all we can do is move bravely towards the joy of each fleeting moment, never knowing which will be the next, or the last.

I lay my head on Kelly's lap while she stroked my hair for a while. I walked to the diving board, threw off my bustier and tutu and dove into the pool, hoping the cool water would let me reemerge ready to take on the world. I enjoyed the crisp water against my skin as I let my body float to the surface for air.

January 1, we hopped on a plane back to New York that evening, and I decided to leave the baggage from the past year behind. I had no idea what was ahead of me, but I did know one thing: I was willing to leap forward into the next fleeting moment, whatever it may be.

JAN | MAGIC, UNEXPECTED

"Truth or dare?"

I quietly contemplated the proposition sitting naked in the Jacuzzi tub between the two sexy musicians.

January blew in with a deep freeze and a rush of new energy. Kelly was back at NYU and on the road to law school. She was studying late in the library every night and when she was home, she was either sleeping or buried in her books, scrambling to make up enough credits. I don't think I saw her eat the entire first week of classes.

The play was ten days from opening. It was my most challenging role yet and I was crushing it! I finally had a chance to prove myself to the Off-Broadway theater crowd and, more importantly, to myself. I knew the script inside out. I read it every morning when I woke and every night before bed in its entirety. I meant business and wasn't going to squander my chance to demand respect as a professional artist.

Kelly and I were focused and driven. We didn't have time to think about guys; there was too much to accomplish.

In order for anyone to take me seriously, I had to take myself seriously. I was the only one who could determine my value; no one else possessed that power unless I gave it to them. My value was determined by the way I treated myself and allowed myself to be treated.

When Russell and Peter didn't take my acting seriously, it frustrated me, but *I* wasn't taking it seriously.

I fell for them and got caught up in the excitement each time. With Russell, I had never been in love before. Peter spoiled me in ways I'd never experienced, with trips and gifts, but I set the example that being in a relationship was more important than my creative work. Life was exciting as Henry's assistant and I made good money so I never felt like I was struggling; however, I was nowhere near where I wanted to be, making a good living as an actor, *not* an assistant. Sure, it wasn't waiting tables, but it wasn't why I left home and moved to New York either.

This got me asking myself some hard questions. What was *my* identity? Who did I want to be? I definitely didn't want to be defined as Henry's assistant, or someone's girlfriend or wife. Slowly, my new path came into focus.

Rehearsals were challenging both physically and psychologically. There were several heavy, emotional scenes, a complicated choreographed fight/rape scene, along with other intimate moments and a full-blown love scene. I was working opposite a wonderful actor, Marcus, who I met a few times from being part of the New York theater community and knowing some of the same artsy people. There were six performers, total, in the piece—three men and three women. I had intimate scenes with two of the three men, the love scenes with Marcus, and the violent rape scene with Victor.

Both men were talented, serious actors. It was a privilege to work with such an accomplished cast; they pushed me to step up my game. Both men were attractive in their own way. Marcus was dark and mysterious and on the quiet side, always reading some classic novel in the corner. Victor was outgoing and loved to joke around, which was a relief because he was so convincing as my attacker that I would have been afraid of him if he didn't have such a great sense of humor.

On breaks I'd catch myself fantasizing about one or the other, depending on who I just finished working with. Then, on one peaceful, snowy day before the dress rehearsal, we were all warming up on stage, and I fantasized about being with both of them, *at the same time,* like, from each side, simultaneously. I kept my face down; my thoughts were so dirty I was embarrassed to look at anyone. The fantasies served as good masturbation material, but that's all they were, fantasies. There is no better way to screw up a show than by getting involved with a cast member, or two.

After Peter, I was satisfied with all the experiences I'd crammed into the previous year and all the lessons that came along with them. I made up for some lost time and my number of sexual partners was now at a respectable, more than five less than ten—completely appropriate for a woman my age. No one needed to know it was all in one year. Holy crap! If I kept going at that pace, I'd hit thirty before I hit thirty…and so what? What would be wrong with that? Kelly hit twenty before she hit twenty and I had more respect for her than I did for most people.

We were rehearsing late into the night at the dress rehearsal. The producer ordered dinner for us and had the stage manager run to the corner to grab a couple bottles of wine. As the cast clinked our glasses together, I had an overwhelming sensation—I could feel Sean in the room, somewhere. I knew this was where I belonged and exactly what I was meant to be doing. The show opened to small audiences, but the house started filling up once word got out about the stellar performances and provocative plot. Two weeks into the run we got our first review in *The Village Voice,* raving. I had been in half a dozen plays in New York by then, but this was the best one by far in the biggest theater I had performed in. It was exciting to finally be a part of something worth seeing. I invited everyone I knew; even Henry came to see it. I was embarrassed to invite him to any of my other stuff, they all seemed amateur in comparison. This play was the real deal.

"I can't believe you've worked for me for four years and I never knew," Henry gushed about my performance as he handed me a bouquet of pink orchids. "How can you show up at my office every day when you are sitting on this much talent?" he continued.

That was the best compliment I had ever received.

The play ran Wednesdays through Sundays and I had Mondays and Tuesdays off. I was still working for Henry, but auditions really started picking up. He was more accommodating than ever now that he saw me in action…he had become a fan.

I was walking home from the theater on a Sunday night when my cell rang.

"Hello," I answered.

"Hey beautiful," said the voice on the other end. My heart skipped a beat; I was silent and shocked, I'd know that adorable voice anywhere.

"Are you there? It's Josh, in LA," he explained.

"Josh! How are you?" I tried to cover up that I was emotional… and curious if he had turned nineteen yet?

"I'm coming to New York. I have a show at Irving Plaza on Tuesday night. You have to come."

"Tuesday works. I'll be there."

"I'll leave you a couple of tickets at the door. I can't wait to see you!"

"I can't wait to see you rock!"

"Told ya I'd be in New York. Talk soon."

I hung up the phone smiling.

I went to the show alone because Kelly had to study and whoever I brought I'd end up ditching to hang with Josh eventually; flying solo just made things simpler. I got to the club as they were setting up their gear after the opening band. Even though Josh left me a back-stage pass I didn't go; there was a good chance that Russell was there and I didn't want to risk running into him and his new wife, Candice. He would probably think I was there to stalk him anyway. I walked around the club and found a place to stand where I could see the stage through people's heads.

There was a good-sized crowd for a relatively unknown band, a few hundred people. The lights started flashing and the boys of Wake took the stage, doing their indie rock thing. It was electrifying. The music was awesome and there was a hint of magic in the air. There were some important music people in the audience that night, like Candice's father, who owned the record label and who could choose to make or break these guys, and a few reviewers. Their music spoke for itself. They nailed every song. The crowd went wild for the sound and the girls went wild for them. They had all the key ingredients for success. I was sure these guys were going places.

After the show, I left quickly to avoid running into Russell. I was heading toward Union Square for a snack when Josh texted me: "Where r u? Did u c the show?"

I texted back: "It was amazing, I can't believe I actually know you. Just getting a snack around the corner."

He texted: "Come hang at my hotel, the W around the corner, 40 min, room 1111."

I replied: "c u soon."

When I arrived, I could see Josh in the lobby bar, having drinks with the rest of the band, Russell, Candice, and presumably her father, all celebrating the success of the show. So, this was Candice. I got a better look at her as she put her hand on Russell's shoulder, her other resting on her visible baby bump. She looked close to forty, attractive, and well put together. I made a beeline for the ladies' room and spent the next ten minutes fussing with my hair and putting on lip-gloss. If not for lip-gloss whatever would we ladies do in a crisis? I didn't vomit. After I had a chance to get over the initial shock of it, I didn't care. I was happy I got to see what kind of a manipulative cheater Russell was. I actually felt bad for Candice.

As I exited the ladies room I ran into Josh by the elevator.

"Perfect timing. I was just going up to look for you," Josh said with a wide smile. He threw his arms around me and planted a wet kiss right on my lips. I congratulated him. I was basically gushing like a screaming tween. When I met these guys in LA they were just a bunch of kids playing music, but after seeing them tonight it was clear: Wake was on the road to rock stardom. I was suddenly a little nervous to be around him.

Josh and I got in the elevator and kissed uncontrollably before the doors had even closed. I hadn't necessarily planned on having sex with Josh, but after seeing him I couldn't hold back my desire. My hands wandered down his pants and his up my shirt. We got to his floor and stumbled out of the elevator and down the hallway to his room, unable to stop touching each other. The sex was fast and hard but so necessary. Once we got it over with, we were able to chat and catch up while snuggled under the sheets. Then we continued with a marathon of sexual delight over the next hour. Alas, we were interrupted by Kevin.

"Sorry, kids, I need to get a few things," he joked as he entered the room. "I had already been up here three times and turned around. You two were going nuts."

"Kick-ass show tonight Kevin, you guys blew me away!" I gushed.

"We're gonna hit the Village and explore some shit if you two wanna come," he said as he searched through his bags.

I looked at Josh's phone on the nightstand. It was after midnight, early for New York, but time for me to conserve my energy for the stage.

Josh turned to me. "What do you say, are you gonna show us around? We got some treats if you want to party?" he asked.

"I wish, but I've got to go home and crash. I didn't have a chance to tell you: I'm starring in a new play and I have performances all week. My voice starts to go if I'm not in bed before two a.m.," I explained apologetically.

"You're in a play? Why didn't you tell me? We don't leave until Thursday. I will for sure come see your play tomorrow. Kev, you in?"

"But of course, we *must* see some theater, we are in the city for it after all," he joked in a terrible British accent.

"Really? You guys want to come?" I asked, surprised.

They both nodded, smiling.

"Great! The show is done by ten, so I can show you guys around for a few hours afterwards?" I hopped out of bed and got dressed, not at all phased by being naked in front of Kevin. I had gotten accustomed to changing in front of people backstage for this new role; nudity really wasn't such a big deal to me anymore.

To my delight, Josh and Kevin showed up to the theater the following night. The house was almost full, and the cast was on point. When the final curtain fell, the theater filled with applause. As I walked down to the edge of the stage to take my bow, I could hear Josh and Kevin cheering for me. That was the first time a guy I was romantic with was cheering for me in the audience. It felt spectacular. After the show, they were waiting for me at the stage door with a bright bouquet of yellow roses. I put them in a vase in the dressing room and we continued out into the night.

We first hit some trendy SoHo hot spots. After, we headed to a party where a friend was DJ-ing in the West Village and ended the night at an open mic on the Lower East Side, where Kevin and I recited poetry we'd written. I left the boys with some recommendations for the rest of their stay and excused myself after the open mic ended to head uptown.

I was off work the next day and able to sleep in a bit. I stayed in bed until almost eleven, checking emails and reading *The New York Times* online. Josh texted me just as I was debating whether or not to hop in the shower.

"Wanna come over for some room service? My room has a hot tub and it sure is cold out there…"

"Ur in luck, got the day off," I replied.

"Hurry!" he wrote back.

"K," I replied.

I jumped out of bed and rushed to the bathroom to brush my teeth and rinse off. I was free all day and didn't have to be at the theater until 6:00 p.m. I wanted to get in one more quickie before Josh left. I got myself together, hopped on the train to Union Square and was at his hotel by noon. Josh opened the door to his hotel room, kissed me on the lips and hugged me for a long moment before we sat on the couch and made out for a few minutes. Kevin was still asleep.

"I'm starving, mind if we order now, it'll take like an hour to get here," he asked.

"Sure," I smiled.

While he ordered I took a look in the bathroom at the tub. Josh snuck up behind me in the bathroom and kissed my neck.

"Let's fill her up!" he whispered enthusiastically.

While the tub was filling Josh and I stripped down. We stayed warm in the shower while we were waiting, it was a big tub. We kissed passionately in the shower as warm water rolled off of our skin. Josh turned me around and pressed me up against the shower wall as he slid along my body with his. We soaped each other up and then switched locations. We were settled into each other's arms in the tub with the jets going as Kevin opened the bathroom door.

"Room service?" he smirked mischievously at us.

"Thanks man, I got you a veggie burger." Josh replied climbing out of the tub, he wrapped a towel around himself.

"Let's go eat before it gets cold. We can always fill her back up." He extended his hand to help me out of the tub and wrapped a towel around me, scooped me in his arms and carried me to the couch.

The three of us sat on the couch, munching away.

"Do you write plays?" Kevin asked.

I nodded.

"You should do the plays you write. Like, the play last night was fantastic, but I can tell from your poems, you could write something out of this world."

"Thanks, I'm working on it," I blushed.

"Don't give up, it'll come," he said as his eyes pierced through me.

I snuggled closer to Josh as I nibbled on my arugula and avocado salad in a damp towel.

"Do you guys mind if I hop in the tub for a bit?" Kevin asked. "I'll give it back when you want it. I'm not used to winter."

"We can all hang out in it, it's big enough…" I didn't know where that came from, but I said it.

Kevin shot Josh a quizzical look. After lunch, the three of us were in the hot tub. I was leaning against Josh's chest on one side of the tub and Kevin was lounging on the other side. Spotify was playing in the background and everyone was chill. As I soaked between these two boys, I started thinking about how awesome Kevin was. I never really gave it much thought before, but now that we were all naked in the tub, I couldn't help but check out his body.

Kevin softly teased, "Anyone up for a game of truth or dare?"

Josh and I looked at each other. "You don't have to," he said to me protectively. "But if you want to, it could be fun," he added with a smirk.

#WWKD? Wait a second, I'd been fantasizing about getting tag-teamed all month by the two actors in my play...it was something I was curious about. Correction, new hashtag, #WWDD? - *What Would Dana Do?* I felt comfortable with Josh and Kevin; they treated me with respect and we didn't know any of the same people, except Russell, who I almost wanted to find out, and they lived on a totally opposite coast, which meant the only people who would ever know would be the ones I told.

I was sitting between Josh's legs in the deep Jacuzzi tub, and the jets were on full blast as the bathroom filled up with steam. It felt decadent on a cold winter's day. Josh massaged my shoulders as Kevin massaged my feet and calves. Josh brushed his lips along my shoulders, kissing up my neck, feeling my breasts and squeezing my nipples. Kevin licked his lips as he watched my nipples perk up and stick out. He squeezed my foot harder. Josh turned my chin and kissed my lips slowly, circling his tongue around mine. Kevin floated across the tub next to me and turned my chin towards him, releasing my lips from Josh guiding me onto his. Josh's hands remained on my breasts, rolling my nipples between his fingers as Kevin kissed me deeply, much harder than Josh. I ran my hands up Kevin's chest and playfully scratched down his torso under the water. I could feel Josh's erection against my ass behind me as I remained between his legs with his one hand wrapped around my breast and the other gently teasing my panic button under the water. With my left hand I reached back and stroked Josh, with my right I teased Kevin's thighs under water as his erection danced around, trying to find my hand. That's when we decided to venture from the hot tub to the bed...

Josh once again wrapped me in a towel then carried me to the bed. He lay me down and unwrapped me on the king-sized mattress. He kissed up the length of my body, then stood beside the bed with his erection next to my face and fed it into my mouth. Kevin followed behind and placed a few condoms on the bed. He climbed between my legs and tasted me gently. Josh looked down into my eyes, smiling with approval as he pumped my mouth and gently stroked my head. Kevin slid his tongue tenderly across my treasure as my pelvis rose to meet his attention.

Josh pulled out of my mouth as he noticed me approaching my first orgasm, my body clenched in pleasure. Kevin came up for air and kissed my mouth, pleased with himself.

Josh grinned as he traded places with Kevin between my legs. Kevin knelt by the pillow and turned my head toward him. He stroked himself a few times and looked me in the eye for approval before sliding his tip across my bottom lip. I felt his cream coating my lips as he continued to glide himself inside my mouth. Josh thrust his fingers inside me as he licked me, massaging my G Spot and sending me into orbit. I sucked Kevin as Josh explored my insides with his tongue and fingers. We rotated in several positions, simultaneously pleasuring each other. Josh picked up a condom from the floor, where they all eventually landed.

"So, we should probably talk for a minute before we go any further," Josh said, condom in hand.

I couldn't help but think something was wrong. I sat up.

"What's up, bro?" Kevin asked casually.

"I just want to make sure we are all cool with what's happening, how far we are all comfortable going…"

"Well, that's your call, you two have a thing, I'm kinda crashing in," Kevin rationalized.

"No, I don't mean that," Josh explained as he looked at me. "I mean, Kevin and I are down, we're both really into you. I just don't want you to feel pressure, like you can't say no because we are all already naked."

Wow. Impressive communication skills and self-control!

"Would it hurt your feelings if Kevin and I have sex?" I asked quietly.

"No, I think it would be really cool. Watching the two of you is really turning me on, it's like live porn. But way, way better," he reassured me.

I guess there are situations where the tag team isn't gay.... Like the *rock star tag team*...for them, sharing a chick is like sharing a joint; it's just something they do when they're killing time in their hotel room. Kidding aside, three people who genuinely liked and respected each other had an opportunity to explore something rare and extraordinary, so I decided to forget what other people might think about me hooking up with two guys at the same time...and took a long second to decide what *I thought* about it. #WWDD?

"I'm really turned on too," I said seductively, inviting them both towards me. They each crawled up the bed onto either side of me.

Kevin and I kissed facing each other and Josh was behind spooning me, caressing my back and my legs. I stroked Kevin, getting him ready as he unwrapped a condom and slid it onto himself. He rolled onto his back and I climbed on top of him and lowered myself onto his excitement. I inched my way down as both Josh and Kevin watched me, their eyes darting from my face to my pussy as I took as much as I could, gently rocking back and forth. Josh lay on his back stroking himself as he enjoyed the show. Kevin rolled me over so we were on our sides and Josh was spooning me once again, only this time he was running his finger between my cheeks.

In the past I was frightened to try anything involving the back door but for some reason I trusted Josh and wanted to experience sensations I had never felt before. If he was relationship material, I wouldn't have been so adventurous; I would have been afraid of being judged and shamed for it later on. But I knew Josh wasn't *the one*, so it was the perfect opportunity to experiment. I caught that fleeting moment of magic and I've never regretted it.

These musicians played my body, causing vibrations in areas I was unaware of. I felt like a goddess; I felt worshipped. They were both coming close to finishing, Josh inside me doggy style, while Kevin was in my mouth, when Josh had an idea and started sliding himself between my cheeks. Kevin put on another condom and I climbed back on top of him as Josh got behind me and started sliding himself along my back door while he nibbled my ear. Juice squirted out of me onto Kevin as I slid up and down on him. I was so wet and so aroused my juice lubricated my ass and Josh was able to slide in slowly, inching his way as Kevin was buried deep in my pussy.

"Go slow," I gasped, and I used my hands to try and control Josh's depth and rhythm.

I experienced double penetration for the first and only time. It was the most erotic and empowering sexual adventure of my life. Ultimately, I was presented with what I indeed considered a once-in-a-lifetime opportunity, and I went for it. Let's call it the Grammy Sandwich. Granted they didn't have a Grammy then, but they have two now...

Time ran out, the boys had to get to JFK, and I had to get to the theater. Josh and I snuggled on the bed as we kissed goodbye. I was smitten with him, but he was nineteen and at the beginning of his journey. He had years of sold-out stadiums and world tours ahead of him and still wasn't legal to have a drink for another two years. He held me tightly and whispered in my ear, "You deserve the best, beautiful, don't ever sell yourself short. I saw you last night, the real you. You are a fucking star, now own it."

I went to the theater that night and had an outstanding performance. Every time I set foot on that stage, I kept getting better and better. I put everything I had into it and there was no question where I belonged.

Our last few weeks of performances were completely sold out in advance. Closing weekend, we had to turn so many people away there was talk of an extended run, but nothing was confirmed. I was in the dressing room, cleaning off my makeup and putting my things away after our final performance when there was a knock at the door. Heather, the playwright, and Erez, the director, let themselves in, closing the door behind them.

Erez gave me a warm hug. "You are spectacular! You had a really tough job and delivered beyond our expectations every night. We are incredibly impressed with you," he confessed.

I smiled with tears in my eyes. "Thank you. I'm grateful you gave me a chance."

"We are in negotiations with a big indie film producer and have a deal on the table to make the movie," Erez continued.

My heart raced; I didn't understand what this meant, or if I would be a part of it.

"We're not sure about casting; we have a good-sized budget and are in a position to hire some bigger names," Heather interjected. "You might hear some rumors over the next few weeks. We just wanted to tell you the one thing the producer is sure of is keeping *you* as the leading lady."

I was silent, in disbelief.

"Please keep this to yourself. We don't want to upset anyone until we have more details," Erez added.

"But you…you are the star of this piece stage and screen, no matter what," Heather gushed with tears in her eyes.

I nodded, unable to speak. The world was spinning around me.

"We will see you at the party," Erez added.

They each held me tightly and left me to get changed. I wept in my dressing room until Kelly came in. "Those better be happy tears," Kelly scolded as she entered.

"They are," I explained. "I just don't want it to be over."

"Honey, it's NOT!" She squeezed me tight. "This is the beginning."

We were soon interrupted by a deep smooth voice. "Hello?" I turned around and to my amazement there was Bryce.

"Hi," I said, confused, "what are you doing here?" Although we had a few work conversations, I hadn't seen him since the morning after Henry's birthday.

"I ran into Henry last week and heard that there was this incredible actress in this new play that wasn't to be missed."

"Henry said that?" I asked, smiling.

"No, that's what *Time Out New York* said. Me, I wouldn't know, the show has been sold out for weeks, so I've been across the street waiting for two hours to give these to you." He presented a bouquet of white lilies.

"They're beautiful!" I kissed his cheek gently. I emptied some wilting flowers from one of the vases in my dressing room, kept one petal for my scrapbook and tossed them in the trash, then unwrapped the new lilies and set them in the vase with fresh water.

"Do you want to go for a drink or something?" he asked. "Both of you," he added quickly to include Kelly.

"The cast party starts shortly; I'm sorry, it's not a good time." I wasn't about to give up *my* celebration, today was about *my* success, not about a man.

"Right, I shouldn't have assumed...you're the toast of Off-Broadway and you deserve a party." He took my hand in his and looked deep into my eyes. "I asked Henry if he would mind us dating." He became serious.

I looked at him surprised. "You did?"

Kelly took her cue and excused herself. "I'll be out there waiting. Nice to see you, Bryce."

"I haven't stopped thinking about you since that night in the summer. I can't remember the last time I had that much fun on a date."

"What did Henry say?" I was taken aback.

"He was cool, he figured you wouldn't be working for him much longer anyway," he grinned.

"What?" My heart sank, was he firing me? Did Bryce get me fired?

"He said he'd lose you to Broadway or Hollywood soon enough and told me to go for it."

I beamed. He was still holding my hand firmly, his eyes locked with mine.

"He also said if he was the marrying type he would have wife-ed you by now."

I didn't know how to respond to that one.

"Can I take you to dinner this week when you're free? On a proper date? I know a great, quiet Italian spot in the Village. I can pick you up."

"Yes," I agreed.

Bryce kissed my hand and took his exit.

All that time I'd been searching for love I didn't have a real grasp of who I was or what kind of love I was even looking for. I still didn't have all the answers but was learning that love rarely presents itself in the standard storybook format with palaces and ball gowns…or opera tickets and trips to Paris. It wasn't until I fell madly in love with *myself* that my life started to take shape the way I had always envisioned. All the magic I had been searching for was inside me the whole time. Over my *Year of the Slut* I finally found the confidence to let it out in my own unique way…And then everything fell into place.

ACKNOWLEDGEMENTS

Aron Tanny, you are the biggest inspiration in my life and the driving force of my creative work, you are forever in my heart and I miss you like crazy. Thank you for giving me the confidence to fiercely follow my dreams!

Thank you Patricia Tabone for always believing in me, you are my artistic partner in crime, sounding board and biggest supporter. Not only did you make *Year of the Slut* possible as the Executive Producer of the Solo Show this book was adapted from, you have been with me every step of the way since I began my creative journey in Tony's class.

To my mother Emma, thank you for being the strongest woman I know and teaching me to be fearless, to fight for myself and what I believe in.

Thanks to my father Howard for teaching me how to work hard and "stick with it" no matter what challenges I'm confronted with.

My brother Michael, thank you for being in my corner. You are a great friend and your support and understanding mean the world to me.

Adrienne Jacob, this book wouldn't exist without you encouraging me to write the play and for being one of the first champions of the stage version of *Year of the Slut*, I am grateful for you. I would also like to thank Michelle Danner at Edgemar Center for the Arts for the inspiration to do a solo show and for your guidance when I first worked out the pieces of the play in your acting class.

Thanks to Vandana Taxali for suggesting I adapt my show into a novel; you sparked this endeavor.

Nicola Wheir, thank you for the amazing notes and all the help getting this book in shape. Your feedback has been invaluable and I couldn't have done it without you.

Lee Parpart, my copy editor, thank you for your incredible attention to detail and for getting me to the finish line.

A huge shout out to Stacey Dymalski, *www.TheMemoirMidwife. com*, for your advice and expertise on creating a business plan for this book, I am grateful for all your insight.

Thanks to Sandi Roberts for your help with the cover art concept, and to Cindy Marinangel, and Ashley Gianni for your invaluable input, I couldn't have come up with it on my own.

A very special thank you to Cyndy Spierer for the continued support, encouragement and notes on each draft of the manuscript and to the rest of my squad for notes and feedback: Jillian Earle, Carla Lieberman and Naomi Carniol. Your excitement gave me the confidence to do this.

My darlings Savannah and Scarlett Cohen, your enthusiasm and feedback has kept me excited about telling this story. I love you both with all my heart.

Jeff Murray, thank you for helping me breathe life into the first incarnation of the play *Year of the Slut*. You are a wonderful director and I am grateful you are part of my creative family.

Thank you Dan Fauci for your extraordinary workshop "The Mastery of Self Expression" and for mentoring me on the stage production. I am grateful for all the time you spent giving me notes on the play and your belief in me.

GirandaFace, thank you for giving me the love and support I needed to write and mount my initial productions of *Year of the Slut*. I couldn't have done it without you.

Thanks to my production team for the LA and New York productions of the show: Danielle Hobbs, Vince Tula, Juliet Klanchar, Louis B. Crocco, Dina Paola Rodriguez, Randy Rivera and Kateria Hatton, I truly couldn't have done it without all your talents. I would also like to express my gratitude to Erez Ziv and www.frigid.nyc for the amazing opportunity to perform *Year of the Slut* at your festival and for receiving the Audience Choice Award.

Stewart Till, thank you for your constant support and always championing my work.

A very special thank you to James Kochalka for believing in me and giving me the space to create. You have made this book possible in so many ways and I am forever grateful to you.

Heather Hatton, thank you for exposing me to all the magical worlds of New York City and taking me on so many crazy adventures; this story would not exist without your inspiration.

Dear Reader,

Thank you for joining Dana on her wild year of discovery. I hope you are amused, aroused and inspired by her escapades. If you enjoyed the book we would love to hear from you! Please help spread the word by leaving a review on Amazon.com or Goodreads.com.

Dana's adventures continue in the next book of the "Year of the What?" series "Year of the Bitch." To stay up to date with the series and upcoming events please sign up for our newsletter at www.YearOfTheWhat.com or connect on social media at @iamjenlieberman on Instagram, Facebook, Twitter.

Wishing you many outrageous and fulfilling adventures! Always remember to follow your heart when you're posed with those tough decisions and if you still don't know what to do just think #WWDD (#whatwoulddanado?)

With love and gratitude,

Jennifer

ABOUT THE AUTHOR

Photo: Genevieve Marie Photography

Jennifer Lieberman is from Maple, Ontario, Canada and holds a Bachelor of Arts in Philosophy from York University in Toronto. Jennifer has appeared in over thirty stage productions in Toronto, New York City, Los Angeles, Australia and Europe; including her Award-Winning Solo Show *Year of the Slut*, which this book was adapted from. In addition to her performance career she has penned a number of screen and stage plays including the wacky web-series *Dumpwater Divas* and the short films *Leash* and *Details* which both screened at the Festival De Cannes' Court Métrage among other international film festivals. *Year of the What?* is Lieberman's first novel. *www.YearOfTheWhat.com*

66361363R00128